DEDICATION

*To our faithful and loyal readers.
The voracious readers.
The vacation readers.
The bathroom readers.
We do this for you.
Enjoy!*

RUNAWAY
CASCADE MOUNTAIN MANHUNT

MIA LONDON
SUSAN SHEEHEY

Runaway
Cascade Mountain Manhunt Series
Book One
by Mia London and Susan Sheehey

ISBN: 978-1947874176 (E-Book)
978-1947874190 (Paperback)

Publisher: Amepphire Press
11923 NE Sumner St, Ste 766015
Portland, OR 97220

Edited by Sharon Pickrel
Formatted by Leigh Stone
Cover design copyright © Romance Novel Covers Now

Published in the United States of America

RUNAWAY
ROMANTIC SUSPENSE SERIES, BOOK 1

Sweet-and-sassy Skye in a small mountain town yearns for the adventures in her mystery and suspense novels, but a DEA cyber-security specialist on the run may be more action than she can handle.

CHAPTER 1

"NONE OF THIS adds up, Monroe." DEA Assistant Special Agent in Charge John Bordowski sat across the table, his arms crossed.

Reed buried his head in his hands. The air conditioner buzzed in the upper corner louder than the fluorescent lights overhead. He'd been sitting in this uncomfortable chair in the El Paso debriefing room for three hours. His partner's killer was getting farther away with every second. "What more do you want? I've told you everything I know. I've given you every single file on all my hard drives."

"What about the ones in the safe house you two were using?"

"The cartel suspects caught up with me, and I had to bolt. I got here as soon as I could shake them. I've given you all the backups I have."

"Did you?"

Reed looked up, his eyes narrowing at his boss' accusatory tone. "What's that supposed to mean?"

"You're hiding something. This timeline doesn't make sense. In a three-year operation against the Cabello cartel, the only thing you can show for it is a bunch of useless surveillance files and a dead partner."

Reed winced. This couldn't be happening. Only three

days ago, Joe was alive. If only he'd gotten to that damn warehouse a minute sooner. One fucking minute.

He dropped his head, staring at the table's metal surface covered in scratches. He and Joe had been partners for years. He'd learned everything about the legal side of law enforcement from him. But they were more than partners. They were friends and brothers. They'd celebrated holidays together, played sports and worked out together, and got drunk together. They'd lived in the same damn tiny safehouse for three years straight.

That was all gone in the blink of an eye.

Reed could still hear the echo of the gunshots, and see Joe collapse to the ground like a ragdoll.

Reed drew his weapon, but his killer was quicker and ran before he could get off a shot. Shortly followed by rubber tires squealing on the asphalt.

He held Joe as long as he could. Joe! Joe! Where the hell is backup?

The scene replayed in his head a million times. The metallic smell of the blood, the last second when he'd looked into Joe's eyes before they closed. He'd tried to plug the wounds and stop the bleeding, but it was useless. Blood was everywhere.

Joe! Hang on!

He wanted to put his fist through a wall. He glared at Bordowski. His boss was right about one thing. Joe's recent behavior didn't make any sense. His partner had been meticulous in his reports, a stickler about filing them on time. "I don't understand. He and I were in constant contact, in lockstep this entire investigation. Except for the last few days, I've known his every move, and he knew mine."

"Is that so? Then care to tell me why Joe hadn't filed a

single report in more than a month?"

Reed's mouth went dry. He'd seen his partner write up dozens of reports, right up until the last day he'd seen him. "That can't be right."

"Odd, wouldn't you say? I thought the same thing." Bordowski rolled his pen back and forth on the table between his fingers. "A fifteen-year veteran of the DEA, previously diligent about filing all his other reports, decided to stop sending them in. Not likely. So what's the more probable scenario? That they're getting deleted from our system, which can't happen without top clearance, way above my paygrade. Or perhaps by a very...gifted...hacker."

Reed blinked, finally making the connection. He barely comprehended the implication floating in the air. "You think I deleted his reports from the system?"

Bordowski gave him a knowing stare. "One who is *very* familiar with our systems and security protocols."

A new realization hit him in the face like a vat of freezing acid. "This isn't a debriefing, is it?"

His boss leaned his arms on the table. His expression harsh and unforgiving. In all the years Reed had worked for him, he'd never seen him like this. "I know what you did for a living before Joe brought you into the DEA as a cybersecurity analyst. He said you were the best he'd ever seen. That you can find anyone, that's why we hired you, despite your record. Then just before Joe's murder, magically, you couldn't find him."

"He turned off his car's geolocator and his phone."

"*He* did? Or did you do it for him?"

It took everything he had not to spit in his boss' face. "*He* did it."

"Then why did he go silent?"

Reed restrained himself from growling at the man, and

his voice dropped. "You don't think I haven't asked myself that question a thousand times? He wasn't acting right those last few days. Joe said he wanted to follow a lead on his own. He told me forty-eight hours max. Then he just walked out. The next I heard from him was that night. He texted me to come help him."

"Where you tracked his phone to the warehouse? The phone he'd shut off."

His heart hammered fast, threatening to crack his sternum from the inside out. "He'd turned it back on by then. When I showed up, I saw him talking to two men. One shot him three times in the chest, then ran off. Why aren't you chasing them?"

"Because you're the one with Joe's blood on your hands. Literally."

Reed glanced down at his open palms. Dried blood was still under his nails. From where he'd held Joe in his arms, kneeling on that cold, concrete floor as his partner bled to death. He hadn't managed to wash off the stains beyond a cursory attempt in a gas station bathroom.

He'd never regretted his previous life as a black-hatter, a cybercriminal by the time he was sixteen. That's where he gained all the cybersecurity knowledge he now used for the right side of the law. He viewed those years on the *other side* as necessary industry knowledge and how to crack into uncrackable systems and networks.

But his boss throwing it back in his face and using it as a way to pin Joe's death on him? There was no way the DEA would do that. Not to one of their own. Or at least he thought he was one of them.

Bordowski watched him, studying him, like a scientist observing a lab rat.

Had he been a lab rat this whole time?

"You think *I* killed my partner?" he asked, barely audible. His head pounded. This couldn't be real.

"You're the only one who knew where he kept all his files. They're all gone. You were the last person to see him alive. You were the last person to leave that warehouse where he was killed. You're the prime suspect."

Now the vat of acid climbed up his throat. "Why would I kill Joe?"

"Did you miss your old life as a cybercriminal? Figure being a DEA agent was too boring? Perhaps Joe caught you. You had to cover your tracks, so you set him up. To get taken out by the very men you were investigating."

Reed shook his head. He couldn't believe what he was hearing. "I would never do that to Joe. I owe him my life."

"Yes, you do." His nostrils flared. "Joe was one of our best men. Now, he's dead because of you." Bordowski's mouth twitched with hatred.

A long pause settled between them as the events of the last few hours sank into his mind. The DEA was dropping it all on his shoulders.

His boss reached into his back pocket and pulled out a set of handcuffs. "Hold out your wrists."

He could barely breathe. His lungs caved in on themselves, refusing to expand. He'd risked his life to throw off the cartel thugs trying to kill him for witnessing the murder. Voluntarily returned to the DEA field office to get help in avenging his partner. After everything he'd done and everything he'd seen, and all the years spent next to and learning from his mentor, they thought Reed was the murderer.

"Don't make this harder than it already is, Monroe," Bordowski urged. He stood, pushing back his chair with the back of his knees. "If you surrender quietly, I will do everything I can to help you."

He glanced behind him. Two more DEA agents came in. No doubt to escort him to holding. Whereas a suspected cop-killer, he'd never see the light of day again. Which meant his boss' offer was nothing more than a hoax. To get him to yield. To confess. For something he didn't do.

In a gut-wrenching daze, he complied. The warm metal clamped down on his clammy skin, the clicking noise echoing in his brain.

"I never thought I'd see you like this," his boss muttered like a parent scolding a child. "Joe thought so highly of you."

He stood and absent-mindedly let the agents escort him out of the room and down the hall. Faces passed by him in a blur, some in shock, others angry. But that didn't match the level of shock and anger within himself.

Joe's killer was going to get away.

They were blaming Reed for it.

This was *not* the DEA he knew. This was *not* the justice he worked for tirelessly. They'd once considered his expertise in cybersecurity a highly valued asset, and now they were using it to condemn him.

It didn't matter how innocent he was—he'd get locked away forever. And Joe wouldn't get the vindication he deserved. The whole thing made him want to fuck this whole thing and rage against authority. Just like his younger days.

But his mentor had convinced him he was better than that. To fight for what was right. What was just.

Staring at the metal cuffs on his wrists as he was escorted down the hallway, he would not let this be the end. This is *not* how Joe's legacy would end.

If the DEA wasn't going to search for Joe's real

murderer, then Reed had to do it himself.

But he had to get out of these cuffs first.

He saw the sign overhead for the restrooms. "I'm going to throw up." He feigned a gag.

"Don't give me that," the agent beside him said. "Grow a sac."

Reed feigned a louder gag.

The other agent sighed. "I really don't want that shit in my car."

"Fine," the first one sighed and directed him to the bathroom. They stood outside while Reed dashed inside and pretended to make vomiting noises. He searched around for an exit point. Another door or an air duct. A small window in the corner let in additional light. He might be able to fit through it. If only he could get the handcuffs off.

He searched the bathroom for something to pick the lock. He dug in the trash and found a paperclip. In a few seconds, he had the metal off his wrists, thanks to a trick Joe had taught him. Then he shoved the trash can under the window to get a boost. With a few more vomit noises and toilet flushes to keep the agents at bay, he climbed on top of the trash can and squeezed himself through the window.

Which let him out into a gated parking lot for DEA personnel. A guard manned the entrance's security station. Beyond the fence line was a small strip mall with a few stores, including a cafe on the corner with an outdoor patio. The dry air and strong dirt smell filled his senses. He never expected to welcome the dust hitting his face.

Reed acted as naturally as he could as he strolled through the parking lot right up to the guard. "I'm going to grab a bite from across the street. Want anything?"

The guard gave him a strange look but smiled. "Yeah, a turkey panini and soda."

"You got it." Reed continued past the gate with sure, confident steps. Hopefully, he looked calmer than he felt; his heart rate still harder than a jackhammer.

If he was considered the prime suspect in Joe's death, the only way to clear his name was to bring in the real killer. Since the DEA wouldn't do it, he'd have to go it alone. With the cartel after him, too, he'd have to move fast. Luckily for him, he knew how to disappear.

CHAPTER 2

Eleven Months Later

SKYE FLIPPED THE magazine page from behind the diner's counter. *Faster Way to a Bigger Behind* was the headline of the next article.

"What! Are they crazy? Who wants a bigger butt?" She reached behind, running a hand over her backside, smoothing her waitress uniform. She closed the magazine and tossed it in the trash, and then pulled out her detective thriller novel.

"Skye!" Ralph called from the kitchen. The round man could barely tie his apron around his waist, and his bald head reflected the overhead fluorescent lighting. He could be a stodgy SOB, but deep inside, he was a teddy bear. A crotchety, lonely teddy bear.

"Yeah?"

"Did you make more coffee?"

Seriously? She'd been doing this damn job for over five years—geez! Had it been that long? She knew when to make coffee. But frankly, it didn't matter. The damn diner was empty.

"I'm too swamped serving all the full tables," she called back with a sigh. She flipped to her bookmarked page. She'd already read it several times, but at least it would be more interesting than the crap in that magazine.

I have enough boredom in my life to make monks cry.

"Haha, you're a real comedian," Ralph replied and left her to her book.

Suddenly the bell over the front door rang. Probably Tom and Sylvia for their blue-bird brunch routine every Friday. Without setting down her book, she poured two cups of coffee for the regulars. "Is it prune juice or iced tea today?"

A tall man in jeans and a T-shirt approached the counter. *Not* her regulars. The stranger slipped off his aviator sunglasses.

"Is it sweetened?" he asked, answering the question clearly not intended for him.

His deep walnut eyes peered up at her as he slid onto the stool.

"Hi." She stood upright, closed her book, and slipped it under the counter. "What can I get you?" She cleared her scratchy throat.

"How 'bout a black coffee and a menu."

Menu, right. "Sure." She quickly slid the plastic folder before him and turned to get his coffee. Her heart rate picked up, and she wasn't sure if it was from someone new walking into her world, or that new someone was as fine as peach cobbler on a summer afternoon, topped with vanilla bean ice cream. There had to be a story behind this guy. He was definitely not from Cascade Creek.

Skye was born and raised in this one-horse town. She knew everyone and their business, whether she wanted to or not. That's the way these small, rural places worked. Everyone knew everyone, and secrets never stayed that way.

She set the steaming cup in front of him. "Just passing

through?"

"Looking for work. But I haven't had decent coffee in weeks." He took a long drink and seemed to relax further into his seat. She glanced at his hands as they wrapped around the mug. Rough, strong, with thick skin able to handle hot ceramic.

For a brief moment, he glanced to the left, perhaps looking at the empty place or to look out the window, but the sunlight played off his eyes, making them almost amber.

Wow! How did he get through life without those beauties virally shared on social media?

She licked her lips. "Can you cook?"

He shrugged noncommittally.

"Hey, Ralph," she turned to her boss through the open window separating the counter from the back kitchen. "I found a new short-order cook for us."

She looked back at the tall drink of water sitting at her counter, his smooth chin as strong as his hands. "What's your name, handsome?" she asked.

"I'm just your average guy."

She called to the kitchen. "Guy here says he can cook."

"Be right there," Ralph called through the back.

Leaning an elbow on the blue formica countertop, she whispered, "We lost our cook a few weeks ago. Moved out of state to take care of his elderly parents. Ralph's the owner, been doin' the cookin' around here since. You can tell how well that's goin'." Her chin pointed toward the empty dining area.

The corner of his mouth lifted, exposing the most scrumptious dimple she'd ever seen.

Oh, yes. This day was startin' to look up. Her mind wandered to the possibilities behind this Guy. With his clean clothes, fresh aftershave, and only-slightly-dirty black truck parked in the lot, he wasn't a vagrant. Looking for work in a small town like this, maybe he was just discharged from the military and was desperate for the secluded mountain air. Or a former convict out on parole, having paid his debt to society for life insurance fraud or identity theft. She smiled wider with the idea of a world-renowned author finding a new inspiring place to finish his next best-seller. Reality could never live up to her vibrant imagination, but what else could she do in this small, idle town.

Ralph meandered over to the counter, hiking up the pants on his oversized belly. He stared at Guy for a bit too long. Skye resisted rolling her eyes at his obvious, ancient tactic of trying to size up a man with who spoke first.

"Can you boil an egg?" he finally asked. "How about clam chowder?"

"Sure."

"Great. Start tomorrow, six a.m."

The stranger looked at her, then back at Ralph. "What's the pay?"

"Depends on how good the food is." Her boss went back to cleaning the grill in the kitchen.

She tapped the counter in mock celebration. "Congrats."

"That was my interview? Two menu items?" Guy asked.

Skye shrugged. "Simple needs for a simple man. You got yourself a job, just like that." She snapped her fingers and refilled his coffee.

"Yeah. Looks like." He glanced at her nametag. "Thanks, Skye."

"Anytime."

As she moved around the counter, she felt his gaze on

her while sipping on his coffee. She pretended not to notice, though inside, she was practically dancing. It had been a long time since a fine man like this one admired her. He was polite enough to be subtle about it as well. She forced herself to keep busy than pester him with all the questions in her mind. Her best friend, Lynée, always told her she talked too much, rarely let others get a word in edgewise. At least when she was excited about something.

One of her New Year's resolutions—to hold her tongue more often—lasted less than a week.

"How's the latest Security book?" he asked.

She stopped, soap all over her hands as she rinsed them clean. Then she smiled at him. "You caught me."

His lips twitched like he was about to smile, but he kept his deliberate stare. Almost like he was too cautious to let anyone see a lighter side to him. "Did they reveal who framed the butler?"

There was no holding back her grin. The man was not only familiar with the series but knew the point of the next book. She dried her hands, reached under the counter, and slid the book across the surface. "Find out for yourself."

His eyes widened. "You don't want to know?"

She shrugged. "Already read it. I won't spoil it for you."

Be still my heart. He's a book junkie like me.

"Is that pie any good?" he asked, nodding to the cake stand in the corner case on the counter. "I can't remember the last time I had apple pie."

"Seriously?" Skye slid a slice onto a plate and set it in front of him. "That's worse than any crime in these books." She watched his face carefully as he took the first bite. When he sighed and nearly gobbled it up in a few forkfuls, she grabbed a slice for herself and dived in.

Guy smirked. "Staff are allowed to eat the food in front

of customers?"

Skye cocked her head. "Who do you think made that heavenly pile of sugary goodness?"

This time he gave her a full-blown smile—wide, straight, and beautiful.

Shit a brick wall. Her hand gripped the edge of the counter so her knees wouldn't buckle. It was unfair to have a smile like that while the rest of the world tried to hide resting-bitch-faces.

Guy stood and finished the last of his coffee. "What do I owe you?"

She lifted a palm. "Nope. Free coffee and dessert for employees."

He tucked the book inside his jacket pocket. "Thanks for this. It'll give me somethin' to do at night." He spun around, giving her a view of his gorgeous backside. His jeans hugged his ass perfectly.

He has nothing better to do at night? That's a damn shame. I could give him something to keep him occupied.

Just before he left, he slipped on his aviator sunglasses and gave her another smile. "See you tomorrow."

She exhaled and reached under the counter for her glass of ice water. She needed to cool down with something crisp. It might be time to pull out one of those romance novels she splurged on.

"Welcome to Cascade Creek, Guy," she told the empty diner.

Getting excited over a new stranger in town was a tad depressing to Skye, considering all the novels she'd read of far greater adventures. But *this* stranger made her all giddy inside. She had to share it with Lynée. After clocking out, Skye ran the short distance across the gravel parking lot, down the hill and across the overgrown soccer field to the library. The air was unseasonably warm for early October, so all the trees were still a deep green. But orange, yellow, and red patches scattered across the distant mountains like a Kinkaid painting, signaling the belated oncoming autumn.

Yet this was no time to admire the amazing view. There was gossip to share. Gossip only she knew, which was the sweetest kind.

She panted, trying to catch her breath as she pulled on the library's heavy wood door. She blotted her upper lip and scanned the area for her friend.

Lynée's life-long love for books must have rubbed off on Skye as a child since she was now addicted to mystery novels. Until she could find a way out of this small town, they were her only source of adventure. Except for that brief disaster her first year of college, which she never liked talking about. Her best friend, on the other hand, was completely content with vicarious experiences on the page.

Inside the small library with the smell of old books permeating the air, she found the reference desk empty. From the squeaky wheels of the return cart, her bestie was restacking books in the children's section.

She peered over a short bookshelf, where the strawberry-blonde reorganized the children's fantasy section. "Lynée," she stage-whispered, still panting for air.

"Hi, sweetie. How was your shift?" Her bespectacled friend's long hair was pulled back into a messy bun, and her signature oversized mauve sweater looked as comfortable as her shoes.

"Guess what?"

"What?" Lynée pushed the cart down farther.

"We got a new cook."

Lynée glanced up, readjusting the glasses that kept

slipping down her nose. "Hallelujah. Ralph was one bad meal away from poisoning the entire town."

She was right. God bless that poor man. Good businessman, terrible chef.

"His name is Guy, he starts tomorrow, and," she cupped a hand over Lynée's wrist, "he is *fine*." She drew out the last word. "Kinda serious and doesn't smile much, but great muscles and nice ass. And girl, he reads the Security series! Can you believe it?"

"I like him already."

"I can't wait for you to meet him."

"What brought him to Cascade Creek?" Her friend asked the question innocently, without any hint of doubt.

"I don't know yet."

Lynée chuckled. "*That's* what you're enamored with."

"Seriously, though. Why would he pick this place? There's nothin' here."

Her mouth gaped. "What are you talking about? Besides this lovely establishment, we have a refurbished movie theater—"

"Still looks like a church," Skye cut in.

"The apple festival is right around the corner, and," she pulled a book from the cart's bottom shelf, "we just got the new John Grisham in. Saved it for you."

Skye gasped and hugged the beautiful book to her chest. "You're a saint."

"Of course, the main reason anyone stays up here is that we get the most beautiful colors in nature all four seasons. I think that's something even Mr. Grisham couldn't capture."

"Ugh. Sure, the first time you see it. But after *years* here, you're still hypnotized?"

"Absolutely." She pushed the cart a little farther down,

her signature prim-and-proper smile in place.

Why Skye still bothered to have this disagreement with her best friend after all these years, she couldn't explain. Lynée still loved this town and was perfectly content in her perfectly organized library. It was probably the biggest personality difference between them. Adventure was nowhere near the librarian's hopes, where Skye absolutely drooled over it.

"For a non-retiree, is nature enough of a reason to move here?"

"Maybe he's scouting it out before he brings the family here."

"Unlikely. No ring on his finger."

"Lucky you." Lynée winked.

"It's a start."

Both women chuckled, but her friend grinned and shushed her. "You better get outta here. I have work to do." She pushed the cart into the next aisle and readjusted her glasses.

"You stayed up all night reading again," Skye interjected. "Why else aren't you wearing your contacts?"

"Glasses don't dry out my eyes."

"It's not the contacts, girl. Your eyes wouldn't be dry if you got a full night's sleep for once."

Lynée huffed. "I'm not here to impress anyone but myself. Glasses or contacts, you love me for me, right?"

"Are you saying I'm not important enough for you to impress?" Skye joked. "I'm insulted."

"You like it." Lynée winked again.

"Fair enough. Come over later. I'll make dinner." Skye blew her a kiss, spun around, and headed for home. She had a good feeling about this Guy person. This was going to be the beginning of something great. Or at least interesting.

CHAPTER 3

REED DROVE THROUGH the low hills outside Snoqualamie pass, his eyes drifting to the detective novel sitting in the passenger seat. A year on the run, and this was the first time he had a friendly chat with anyone that treated him like a human being. The first time he actually had an inkling of a reminder of what a normal life was supposed to be like. All because of a waitress with a smile from heaven.

He hadn't intended to give her a false name, but when Skye had started calling him Guy, he ran with it. Probably better to keep his real name a secret for the time being. From his days as a black hat cyber junkie, he wouldn't have thought twice about concealing his identity. That was a necessity. But years working on the right side of justice beside Joe had taught him a new appreciation for honesty and integrity. Using a false name now left a bad taste in his mouth. But once again...necessity. To keep the DEA and the cartel off his ass a little while longer.

The scent of fresh apples hung in the air through the open window as he passed by the orchards this area of Washington was known for. The trees looked ripe for harvest. Just the way he remembered. The last time he was here, he was only nine, on a fishing trip with his uncle. The smell was just as strong as then.

There was no way the agency could find him out here—not a single mention of Washington on any file. He'd made sure of it.

Which would give him the time he needed to find out who the hell killed his partner. Because despite what the DEA claimed, it sure as shit wasn't him.

The cabin he rented was far off the beaten path, with only a dirt road leading up behind a big hill. The small place would suit his needs well enough to conduct his research. No one came back here unless they were searching for it, and the tall trees hid the cabin from the main road. After he moved everything inside from his truck, he'd start scoping everything out for access points, hiding places, and a decent sniper's perch.

He counted his paces from the end of the dirt path to the front porch. Thirty, with another ten paces from the bottom step to the front entrance. The old-school latch creaked loudly as he opened the solid wooden door. The room smelled stale and moldy, and dust floated freely in the air like it owned the place. The living room furniture circled the only fireplace in the house. The arrangement meant for functionality and comfort. He'd have to move things around to make it more suitable for a quick getaway, if and when he needed to.

The water was clean and soft, and the kitchen spacious enough. The bedroom at the back of the hallway had a connecting bathroom with a stand-up shower, both tiny. But they were vast improvements from the places he'd laid up in the last year. Hell, he'd spent an entire month outdoors, with three cartel hitmen on his ass, jonesing to finish him off like they did his partner. Hotels were out of the question. Most of them required identification and credit cards, which were too easily tracked. The rest, he was too afraid the locals would give him up. Those cartel bastards had infiltrated everyone.

He stashed his stuff in the front closet and started hiding a few weapons around the cabin, dusting off a few places as he went. Like the small, wooden table that only seated two people. More than big enough for just him. He duct-taped a Ruger under the table, aimed at the door. Another he stashed in a kitchen drawer next to the sink. A rifle behind the fridge, and a few more places. He'd need to get more ammo from town because what he had wasn't nearly enough. At least he always had his K-bar knife tucked in a sheath at his ankle.

As soon as everything was in its place, he started setting up his computer equipment. He doubted this little hunting cabin had Ethernet or other cables to connect to the web, but he came prepared. Satellite hookups would work well. His former life came in handy at times. His life before DEA undercover work.

His partner had often mocked him as a computer geek, a slave to his laptop and the Internet. All playful banter meant to lighten the mood in their often stressful line of work. Countless times, Joe had returned to find Reed still in his computer chair after a full day and forced him to stand up, get a shower and eat. Hell, he probably would've never seen daylight without his mentor urging him to unchain from the chair.

Slave was right. An unfortunate, necessary one to bring down these bastards. He refused to give up. Maybe after all this was over, he'd promise to become an outdoorsman. Go hiking, fishing, and all that Mother-Nature-y stuff normal people enjoyed.

The sun dipped below the treeline, and stars twinkled overhead by the time he finished installing the last security camera outside the back door. The old propane tank for the gas heater was a little closer to the house than he liked. But he didn't have a choice.

His energy waned. Either from the lack of food or fatigue from the road life catching up to him, he wasn't sure.

Clam chowder. That sounded pretty damn good right now. He chuckled. Between all his gap jobs over the last year, a short-order cook was never one of them. But he'd learn. More importantly, somehow, he knew Skye would make the job at least tolerable. Her eyes reminded him of the dark blue storm clouds that rolled through El Paso. Rare, full of lightning that dazzled as much as it brought hope to a desert. That made everyone stop what they were doing to admire it, and equally fear it. Not that he was afraid of Skye, but she was certainly worth the attention.

He glanced at the time. An hour to master clam chowder. What's the chance that spunky waitress even touched the stuff?

Guy set a bowl of clam chowder down in front of Skye. A proud smile on his face. "What do you think?"

Steam rose off the creamy goodness, beckoning her to try a bite. She stopped refilling the napkin holders and used the spoon on the adjoining plate to taste, blowing on it first. The spices hit her in just the right way, warming her insides.

"Mm. What is that, paprika?"

His grin widened. "That's a secret."

He turned back around, retreating to the kitchen.

Skye watched his every step. She'd been watching him all morning. How could she not? The man was even more handsome than the day before with a fresh shave and his hair tucked under a black Seahawks ballcap. Or maybe her imagination was just getting away with itself. It's not like there were many dating options in this town. At least none she hadn't known most of her life and wasn't interested. Besides, not many men could pull off that cooking apron the way he did.

"Skye, more coffee, please?" Gloria asked from the corner booth.

She jumped. "Oh! Sorry!" She grabbed the pot and cringed on the way over to her tables. They'd asked for refills a while ago, and she kept getting distracted. Gloria sat beside her new love-interest, Principal Foster. Rumor had it she and Victor had been seeing each other a few weeks now. Which was kinda interesting since Syke thought Victor was gay. But at least now the diner was back to half-full. Rumors had spread throughout town about the new cook, and people were anxious to see if he was worth his salt. Thank God for that. She wouldn't have to look for a new job while she finished her college courses.

Skye glanced back at the counter where Guy had set another three breakfast plates. He wore a concentrated prideful expression. Only one plate had been sent back this morning, with someone's eggs a little too runny. Otherwise, all the other dishes had been spot-on. Yeah, definitely worth his salt in her mind.

The few interactions he'd had with customers, Skye listened intently. Everyone asked him where he was from and what brought him to town. He had a different excuse for each one: in the witness protection program, a cybercriminal robbing banks from his computer, even a federal agent looking for his next target. Everyone chuckled. His fresh sense of humor was like a warm breeze through this place. Or more like an adrenaline shot to the soul.

Even Gloria and Victor found him instantly charming. Her former principal was impossible to impress, and she rarely saw him smile. But with Guy, the man had chuckled.

She finished washing a set of lunch plates after their last customer. Guy wiped down the grills and restocked ingredients for tomorrow, all the while whistling a song she couldn't identify.

"You seem to be a big hit on your first day."

He shrugged. "Guess people are just grateful not to have to suffer through Ralph's food anymore." Then he continued whistling.

"There are lots of places to become a cook. What brought you into town?"

Guy stopped whistling but continued scrubbing the prep area. His jeans hugged his ass nicely but were relaxed around his thighs. Skye secretly enjoyed the view.

"Are you a doomsday prepper, convinced the apocalypse is around the corner?" She leaned against the counter, her arms braced behind her.

That made him stop cleaning, and he turned to face her. "A what?"

She smiled. "Or are you a cult leader on the run from the authorities?"

The corner of his lip pulled up. "Bank robber on the lamb. Don't tell anyone."

She bit her lip playfully. "I can keep a secret."

"That's pretty rare for a small town. And an imagination as vivid as yours..." He stepped forward. He didn't stop until he was mere inches from her face.

Her heart jumped in anticipation. Was he really that forward, after just one day? Her mind told her to be cautious, but her heart was so damn curious.

Then he reached behind her, his arm brushing against

her hip as he grabbed her novel from under the shelf. "I assume you get that imagination from the likes of Grisham." He flipped through a few pages. "Who else do you like to read?"

Skye's deep breath felt like a gasp. Warm fuzzies filled her all over, which she had to shake from her senses. "Um...King, Steel, Patterson, Roberts. Really I like all fiction, but especially suspense and mystery." Her face was so hot; it was probably beyond red. Damn, he was still so close and smelled like rosemary. "Do you have a lot of time for reading?"

He set the book back on the counter. "Not much lately. But hopefully, I'll have more time now that I'm here."

She was still out of breath. "Well, let me know what you're looking for. I have an insider at the library."

Straight white teeth showed through in his smile. "Does your dealer have the latest Milton book?"

"I'm sure she could oblige. What else are you looking for?"

He thought for a second, his gaze still perusing her face.

Let's see if he takes the bait. What else are you looking for? Something sweet?

"Now that you mention it..." he replied. "There is something I've wanted to sink my teeth into."

She held her breath because his gaze was so disarming. Hypnotizing, even.

He's taking the bait. He likes sweet. Oh, please, take a bite.

"Online gaming."

Skye's trance broke. "What?"

"Online video games. Do you play?"

She huffed out a laugh, trying to hide a hint of

disappointment. "No. Can't say I have."

He pulled off his apron and leaned against the counter beside her. "I hear it's all the rage. Figured I'd give that a shot, too. While I had the time."

She turned her body to face him, her hand on the counter. More to steady herself from his alluring stare. "You came up to Cascade Creek to play online video games?"

He shrugged. "They say there's serious money in it." His lips twitched into a smile. "Where else can a bank robber hide his stash?"

"You could never be a bank robber."

He tilted his head. "Why do you say that?"

"You're too good looking. You'd stick out. The first rule is to blend in ... you know, easily forgettable."

He leaned in, his eyes twinkling with amusement. "You think I'm good looking?"

She rolled her eyes to hide a smirk. "Don't let it go to your head."

"Too late." He winked and spun around, hanging his apron on the hook by the door before he left the diner, the door jingling behind him.

Skye buried her face in her hands. Sure enough, her skin was as hot as a pressure cooker. Well, Lynée was right about one thing.

The enigma of Guy had her completely hypnotized.

CHAPTER 4

THE PROFESSOR'S VOICE in Skye's Corporate Communications and Public Relations class droned on like a robotic feed from a CB radio. She was lucky her mind only wandered instead of being put to sleep by the monotonous white noise. At least now, she had something more intriguing to let her mind wander toward. Images of Guy kept popping up in her brain. He had grace and ease in Rock Road's kitchen, a self-confidence the likes of which she wasn't used to seeing. Of course, she had to hold back a laugh when he couldn't find the switch to the vent hood, and the place started filling with smoke. Ralph almost had a conniption over that.

He circled in her imagination like a brain teaser. *What is he doing here?* Maybe he was broke; Cascade Creek was a cheap place to live. Or perhaps he was running from the law. Or he just got divorced.

Ugh. That last thought unsettled her. Statistically, it was the most likely answer.

Dammit, Skye, enough.

She hardly knew the man, and now she was filling her fantasies, acting like a teenager drooling over his muscles or giggling at his jokes, which is the same behavior that got her burned the first time.

Am I ever going to learn my lesson?

"Miss Winters."

Her attention instantly switched to high alert as the professor called her name.

"Welcome to the discussion. What is one of the things a company can do to dispel a rumor?"

"Um...communicate with people." *Hopefully, not using the voice of a robocaller.*

"Very good. Rather than staying quiet and pretending that nothing is going on, it is essential we communicate with others. The company should approach the rumor mongers themselves and inquire about what they've heard."

Skye exhaled. *Dodged a bullet.* If she could stay focused long enough to finish this class and one more after that, she'd have her degree. How to fill her idle energy with something other than Mr. Sexy Ass at the diner?

She groaned inside.

How Reed had managed to work through his first shift without poisoning anyone with salmonella, he had no idea. Either through his novice abilities at cooking, or constant distraction of Skye's energetic persona, those swaying hips, and intoxicating laughter, someone was bound to have ended up with raw chicken or fish at some point. Or a burnt steak that looked like a hockey puck. Had to be a miracle.

But at least something had gone his way for once in the last year.

He needed to use this new streak to his advantage, capitalize on it for his investigation while he could.

He drove through the small town and back roads for much longer than necessary, making sure to take a different route home. Just in case someone followed him. Old habits and all. Despite all his glances in the rearview mirror, he didn't notice anyone suspicious. But he knew better than to let down his guard. Finally, he pulled up the gravel driveway to his rental house.

He sat in his truck for a few moments. Scanning the outside of the cabin, waiting for something in his gut to warn him. He even scanned the trees, checking for snipers or broken branches they'd left in their wake. Those cartel suckers were slicker, and he couldn't take any chances. But everything seemed just as he'd left it, down to the awkward tilt of the lampshade. His other safeguards were in place, and he deemed it safe to go in.

With a grip on his pistol in the back of his waistband, he ventured inside.

The cabin was quiet. Dust particles illuminated by the sunlight floated in the air. The large twig he'd left on the wooden planks just beyond the door remained unmoved from intruders. His security cameras didn't show anyone snooping around his place while he was gone, either. Always a good sign, he could stay another day. With a deep breath, he uncocked his gun.

A quick shower and change later, he was back in his truck with his laptop bag headed for Seattle. The three-hour drive was a necessity to conduct his first online search. He couldn't make the mistake of doing that from his cabin without the proper proxy equipment in place to hide him from prying eyes. The agency would detect him in three heartbeats, have a pinpoint on his geographic location in minutes, with agents up his ass sooner than he could warm a microwave meal. Not to mention the cartel had their own tech team jonesing for his head in a duffel bag. He was no rookie. Better to do this far from home, at least for now.

Granted, the tactics took a lot more time and involved

more effort, but he had to stay free long enough to identify and find Joe's killer, which was worth more than the additional strain.

The long drive gave him more than enough time to think about his current predicament. To stew over the fact that in the last year, he hadn't gotten any closer to finding his target, bringing them to justice for his partner's death, or at least clearing his own damn name. By the time he'd lost the cartel thugs tailing him and felt comfortable enough to set down a base camp to start his investigation, they'd find him again. Which normally ended up with several bullets flying over his head, and another few weeks in the wilderness trying to throw them off. The only civil conversation he'd had was with the few people in this new town—Skye, in particular.

Please let this place be far enough away. Let me take a deep breath for once.

He passed rows and rows of apple trees, olive trees, and up into the mountains where the pines towered over the road. The fresh air grew crisper with the elevation, and soon he reached Snoqualmie Pass, the point through the Cascade Mountains that led into the western coast of Washington State. Snow already covered the highest point of the barren peaks, though just a light dusting compared to what he remembered in the winters.

Hopefully, he wouldn't be here that long. He could do his clandestine investigation and somehow bring his partner's killer to justice and prove he wasn't a murderer. But he had to be realistic. It would take time to find the information he needed, the evidence to prove it, and more importantly, find where these suckers were located because they were no amateurs. Which meant he had to prepare for a long-haul, including a snowed-in winter in his cabin. God willing. And daily shifts with Skye Winters, with her ocean blue eyes staring at him, eager for him to share something interesting. What he wouldn't give to be snowed in with her for a weekend.

Damn, he had to stay focused. Somehow.

The dark waters of Seattle's Elliott Bay glittered from the snippets of sunlight piercing through the clouds. A breathtaking view if he'd ever seen one. Reed much preferred this part of Mother Nature's beauty than the dry, dusty deserts of El Paso and New Mexico, enchanting as they were.

He made sure his fake mustache, reading glasses, and backward ballcap were properly in place before he found a coffee shop close to the bay. Sporty-hipster facade in place, he settled into a cozy corner. With his laptop open and a fresh venti coffee, it took less than five minutes to find someone with an unlocked wifi signal he could borrow. Using his masking software, he piggy-backed off their I.P. address to check old email accounts and find any information he could about that horrible night eleven months earlier. He combed through news articles, dark web sites, and anything else he could think of to find a lead to chase—a starting off point to dive in further. The real meat of what he needed was behind sophisticated, ironclad security systems within the DEA, NSA, and their top clearance contractors, which would take weeks or months to access, if at all. And he certainly wouldn't dare attempt breaking in from a public coffee shop.

He only had two things to go on: the face of the cartel thug who'd shot his partner, and the single phrase Joe had said with his dying breath: "Dark Inferno."

The man had choked on his own blood as he'd said them. Reed had never seen his mentor's face so ashen, like a ghost, the dark red blood covering his teeth and a trickle-down his chin.

No. He rubbed his temples, trying to shake the image from his mind. "Don't focus on that," whispering to himself, "don't go there."

The son of a bitch who'd killed Joe in cold blood didn't have a name yet. Before the DEA had deleted Reed's logins, he had scanned through all the files to see if anyone matched who he saw in that dark warehouse that night in El Paso. Zilch. But there's no way he would ever forget that man's face. His vicious gleam of sick pleasure after shooting Reed's partner in the chest. The sound of Joe gasping for breath, choking...gurgling...

Shit! He slammed his hands on the table, causing a few patrons to glance his way.

Why hadn't Joe checked in those last few days? Why did he have to go chase that lead on his own? Why hadn't Reed pushed back hard enough on his partner's determination to go it alone? Their case had stalled over the preceding weeks, and Joe had been just as frustrated as Reed. The cartel had found a new way to coordinate drop locations for their drug shipments, completely under DEA radar. Reed and Joe had been thwarted time and again, and they were losing the war against this violent and savvy cartel. Until Joe had finally gotten a nibble of a lead and chased it down on his own. Three days later, Reed had caught up with him in time to see three bullets plugged into his chest.

Dammit, stop it. I'm no good to him as a puddle of PTSD bullshit.

Sure, Reed hadn't had more than three hours of straight sleep since that night. But he could sleep when he was dead. For now, he had work to do—blood to wash off his hands.

He pinched the bridge of his nose. He needed to focus. He couldn't let the emotional anguish distract him.

Dark Inferno, he thought. He didn't even have time to chase down that lead before two more cartel thugs had caught up with him at their safehouse. He only had time to grab his bailout bag filled with cash, a few hard drives, and a few fake IDs—everything else he had to leave behind. With more bullets flying past his ass, there was no time to grab his laptop. Twenty-four hours later, he was sitting in the DEA El Paso field office, waiting for debriefing when they came in and slapped handcuffs on him. They charged him with the murder of his partner and a host of other allegations. They thought he was a double agent. The world spun around him, and he knew the only chance he had was to run.

He'd been on the run ever since, hiding out in one hell hole after another, trying desperately to stay ahead of the agents on his tail and the hitmen with a hard-on for an undercover DEA agent.

After a messy close call in Ruidoso where he'd had to put a slug in two more cartel grunts, he'd gone completely off-grid. No hotels, no major highways with traffic cameras...and no Internet.

A pair of college girls with their caramel macchiato monstrosities walked by him. One gave him a wink and lingered at the napkin and sugar station. In just a quick glance, he knew both their names from their cups, the university they attended from the logo on their cut-off shirts, and what kind of car she drove from her keychain dangling from her hand. Another glance, and he knew her license plate number from the bright yellow Kia out front. He shook his head. Literally in less than three seconds, and he'd know everything about Mariah and her friend, down to their physical addresses, social media accounts, emails, and even their most frequented hangouts from the geolocation information stored on each photo in her account.

He'd learned some pretty shady shit in college, and then even more disturbing tricks in the agency. If he could do it that easily with just the laptop in front of him, these girls didn't want to know what the more nefarious technogeeks like him could do with his full equipment. They'd never take another picture again, let alone touch a computer.

But that's why Reed was in this job. That's why he stuck around. So he could stop it. So he could stop the guy who'd killed Joe and keep more of these evil bastards from hurting anyone else.

He typed 'Dark Inferno' into the search bar.

An online gaming app showed up first. Reed tilted his head. The site seemed like another run-of-the-mill sniper game, similar to ones he played in high school and college. A new one of these games popped up every other week. It wasn't out of the realm of possibility that Joe had played the game to pass the ample downtime they had during their case, but why would he choose this game to be his last words?

Reed entered anything he could think of for Joe's login and password. Scouring his memory for anything his partner might've used as a gamer ID. The man was too smart to use any personal info like middle name, birth date, or anything related to their real identities. After several tries, nothing worked. He'd have to dig further, try to crack some of his old cloud files to see if there was any mention of a login ID or password Joe used, which would potentially put the agency on his tail much quicker than he wanted. But he'd have to save that search for another day. His energy was draining, and the sun was setting, bringing in a beautiful twilight over Elliott Bay. The three-hour drive back was going to be a long one in the dark.

Time to order a coffee-to-go.

CHAPTER 5

DIEGO HUERTA STOOD silently with his arms crossed as he watched his uncle put a bullet into the temple of one of his youngest henchmen. Brains and blood splattered against the barn siding, a good distance from the hacienda in northern Mexico's hills. The large compound housed the main family and extended familiars, along with at least two dozen other henchmen and their families. In the center courtyard between all the smaller buildings, children played with sparklers and pop rockets, masking the sound of the gunshot.

By the time the man's body crumpled to the dirt, Carlos Cabello, the cartel boss, and Diego's eldest uncle, had already turned to Emilio, his second-in-command, and grabbed the outstretched handkerchief to wipe the gun residue from his hands. And the sweat from his brow.

Diego didn't move an inch nor showed a split second of disgust or remorse. All of that had been beaten out of him as a kid. In fact, he now relished this. The man had committed an honest mistake, losing a half-million dollars at the border crossing. For the honesty part of it, the cartel gave him mercy with a quick, clean death. If he'd been stupid enough to attempt stealing from Cabello, or worse, snitching, his death would've been much more painful, prolonged over hours or days. And much more inventive.

All the men in this dirty circle of lifetime gang members were hardcore killers. Doing what had to be done in their vicious business. For Diego, it was the family business.

The only thing that may have saved this man from the cartel's justice was blood. Blood of the Cabello family that ran through Diego's veins. His father was Carlos's brother. Illegitimate or not, blood was blood.

"Send his mother money to pay for the funeral," Carlos instructed Emilio with casual indifference as though he were asking for extra salsa with his meal. "And a little more to cover her rent the rest of the year. Then bring his younger brother into the compound. We must groom a replacement."

And keep a hostage to ensure his mother's silence. Diego's lips curled into a small smile. He knew that tactic well. He was brought to this very compound at the age of ten, after his mother's death. Only her crime hadn't been as simple. She'd fallen in love with the cartel boss's brother and gotten pregnant. Only when she'd learned her lover was in the cartel, she fled to the United States, gave birth to his bastard son, and tried to raise him in secret.

But the cartel finds everyone.

At first, he was angry at being taken from his mother. Then he realized what real power his father's side of the family held. And he devoted his life to learning how to harness it.

"Wipe that smile off your face." Carlos scowled at him. "This is business, not a game. Seems the longer you work for me, the harder it is for you to tell the difference."

"I'm honored you would include me in more important matters than just my usual coding and virtual killing."

The man's cold gaze met his. He tossed the handkerchief on the ground. "Every link in our chain is important—each one with their own specialty and strengths. The games you design are crucial to our family's operation. Your talents are far too valuable to lose with the dirtier aspects of this process. But it's still important for you to learn the consequences should members of our organization fail."

Diego didn't miss the underlying threat but didn't acknowledge it either. He followed his uncle to the side of the barn, the old man walking slowly as he surveyed his private kingdom of beautiful desert hills and a glorious sunset. The rest of his henchmen remained where they were, always scanning for threats, including among themselves. Not that Diego feared any of them. He was more than capable of defending himself.

He'd been groomed from the second he arrived at this hacienda as a scrawny *chamaco* to be part of the cartel. His father had died of a heart attack before he'd ever met him. An ironic death, considering the dangerous nature of his "day job." Diego's father had been addicted to tequila, fatty foods, and sex, in every order possible. During one of his weekend binge-fests, he'd collapsed mid-thrust on top of his mistress. Or so the other kids in the compound had retold him repeatedly during his first few months.

Only when his uncle realized how smart Diego was and how quickly he'd caught on to the way of things—the "kill or be killed" mentality—did he consider using him for more ambitious endeavors. And not just because he had a US passport. Those were like gold down here. Easy access back and forth across the border. Invaluable to a cartel with millions of clients on the other side of the Rio Grande, and billions funding their lifestyle.

Diego had something special. An innate survival instinct he'd inherited from his father, combined with an affinity for coding. So they sent him back to the USA for high school. Then Cal-Tech. All under his alias, Daniel Huerta, who now held two degrees in application development and business supply chain management. He quickly became one of Carlos Cabellos' most coveted assets.

Diego was determined not to follow the same reckless lifestyle as his biological father. He had much higher ladders to climb.

As two men started dragging the dead body into the barn, his uncle turned his back and addressed Diego directly. "How is the next app's development coming along?" He pulled a cigar and lighter from his breast pocket, the end already cut. He took his time lighting it.

"Beta-testing starts next week. If all goes well, should be up and running next month."

Carlos blew a giant puff of smoke over Diego's shoulder. "I still don't think we should abandon the first game you developed. It's been working marvelously for our efforts."

"You always say stay several steps ahead of our enemies. If they ever catch on to our latest methods, we have an alternative in place. With a legitimate side-income stream."

His uncle eyed him, his dark eyes troubled under his bushy eyebrows. Time and violence had weathered the old man like a used leather chair. "Speaking of our enemies, you still haven't found that *pinche* DEA agent. It's been a year."

Diego's insides filled with fire. "His trace ran cold. Last we heard of him he was running up the desert through New Mexico. He's living off-grid. But sooner or later he'll pop up. If anyone can track him, I can. We'll take him out then."

Carlos moved in suddenly, with surprising deftness for his advanced age. "*I'll* take him out," he growled. "You won't move one toe out of your little cave."

Diego growled right back at him. He was the only one who even dared. "I can do more than just wreak havoc on a keyboard. Haven't I proved that in El Paso?"

"You stepped out of line in El Paso," his uncle snapped. "I'd have killed anyone else for disobeying my orders. Had you done as you were told, we wouldn't have this rogue agent still on the loose."

"I was the one who found that *pinche gringo* snooping around the game. Without me, DEA would've raided this compound, making a *piñata* out of your ass in federal prison."

Carlos's eyes darkened, and his whole face flushed with rage. In a split second, he'd cupped Diego's face in his hands, squeezing his cheeks together and dragging him down a few inches to stare down into his face.

Diego's heart nearly stopped. His uncle was the only man he was truly afraid of.

The burning end of the cigar was merely a fraction of a millimeter from his eye. "Do not forget yourself, *Diegocito*. As valuable as you are to me, everyone is replaceable. Your time will come. When you learn patience. I still see the scrawny *pollito* too good to piss in the dirt." He released his nephew's face.

Diego rubbed his jaw, huffing out a breath to control his temper.

"I have my own protections from the Americans," his uncle continued. "You think I wouldn't, after all this time? Dare threaten me again, *niñito*, and I'll feed you to the wolves myself." His uncle spat on the ground by Diego's feet and tossed his cigar into the bushes. With a last glare, he turned and strolled back up to the hacienda, his hands in his pockets, like a fucking monarch who just finished washing his hands.

"You're right about one thing," Diego muttered, well out of his uncle's earshot. "Everyone is replaceable. Even you."

CHAPTER 6

SKYE NORMALLY LOVED Sundays. She could sleep in and study for her degree, just six credit hours away. This particular one rewarded Cascade Creek with sunny, warm temperatures that others would take advantage of by enjoying nature before autumn set in. Her best friend would spend most of it in church.

But this particular Sunday, Skye hated it. The diner was closed. That meant she didn't get to see Guy.

In the two weeks since he'd started working there, she was completely intrigued by him, drawn to him. Many of the customers were too. She'd been asked so many times if she knew where he came from, or why he chose Cascade Creek to settle down in. Unfortunately, she couldn't answer their questions. But she was as equally curious. Maybe because he was so fine to look at, and it made her day go by faster. Perhaps it was because he was new, and she still hadn't learned much about him, which gave her imagination permission to roam freely into amazing, albeit improbable territories.

Perhaps it was because she started to feel a little more alive with him there.

Whatever the reason, his absence with a closed diner made Sundays more acutely depressing.

How did he spend his days off? Hiking? Fixing up old houses? Perhaps reading an expansive library?

The whole day crawled by slowly, until finally—thankfully—Monday arrived. She practically leaped out of bed and spent extra time doing her hair and makeup, putting a little more accentuation into her eyeliner and dusty rose shadow to brighten against her light gray waitress uniform.

She pulled into the Rock Road Diner's parking lot to see Mr. Nice Ass and his black truck already there. Her heart skipped a little. With a quick look in her rearview mirror, she fluffed her hair and took a calming breath. As she shut her car door, she noticed a few holes in the bottom of Guy's rear fender. Small ones, in perfect circles that couldn't be from rocks kicked up off the road. Like BB gun pellets, perhaps.

Hm.

Maybe he was an outdoorsman. Perhaps he'd spent yesterday hunting. But if he was a hunter, why would he use only a BB gun? This was certainly the right area of the country for those who loved nature. Is that why he chose Cascade Creek?

Good God, can't my brain just be quiet for ten seconds?

She went inside.

The man was switching on all the lights and starting up the grills. When the jingling bell above the door pulled his gaze to meet hers, his lips quirked up.

"Morning. You're here early," she greeted him.

He wore his ballcap backward again, and a few wrinkles crossed his SeaHawks shirt. A subtle layer of scruff covered his chin.

"Want some coffee?" She stuck her purse under the

counter behind the napkin refills and flipped on the coffee maker.

"Love some."

"Black, no sugar, right?"

He grabbed his apron from the hook on the wall. "Good memory."

"You still haven't told me why you're in Cascade Creek, by the way." Hopefully, the quiet time together without others around would entice him to open up more.

He pursed his lips, pausing as he tied his apron strings. "I'm a former secret agent investigating a murder."

She stopped dead in her tracks, holding an empty mug while the coffee dripped into the pot. With the most serious expression she could conjure, she replied, "The bodies were already there when I moved in."

He blinked. The apron strings fell from his fingers.

Skye couldn't hold the farce, and let the laugh explode from her chest. "Dangit, I would suck at a lie detector test."

"That's a good thing," he chuckled. "'Cuz then I'd have to take you in. Good thing I left the handcuffs in my other getaway car."

She snorted and poured a fresh cup of coffee for him. "You almost had me with that video game malarkey the other day." She playfully punched his upper arm. "One of these days, you're gonna tell me the truth. I already know you can't be a secret agent."

His smile faded behind a sip of his coffee. "Why, I'm too good-looking again?"

"You have horrible aim with a BB gun." She started refilling the salt and pepper shakers.

He gave her a strange look. "BB gun?"

"The holes in your rear fender. From a BB gun, right? A real hunter knows not to aim the weapon at their own truck." She chuckled and kept working.

Guy cleared his throat. "Why are you in Cascade Creek, Skye? Born and bred here, or are you just really into mountain men?"

The salt spilled from filling a shaker. She set it down and grabbed a napkin to wipe it up. For a moment, she forgot he wasn't a native. Everyone already knew the reason she'd come back to Cascade Creek, and most were kind enough to spare her the retelling. Despite the all-American mentality of this small town, everyone here had skeletons. Except hers just wouldn't stay in the damn closet like everyone else's.

On a deep breath, she left the salt shaker on the table to pour her own coffee with extra cream and sugar. "Let's just say I got the nerve to leave town for college only to be burned my first year out. Badly."

"A boyfriend?"

She stirred her coffee a little too hard. "I hate being predictable."

He shrugged. "Sorry to hear that. Nice ones always seem to get burned."

She sipped her coffee, hoping if she blushed, she could blame it on the hot caffeine. She hadn't expected that compliment. "Maybe I shouldn't have been as nice."

He shook his head and took a step closer. "He shouldn't have been an asshole. Whoever he is. You never change who you are, especially not for an asshole."

She smiled over the rim of her mug. "How insightful, doctor. You should start your own self-help podcast. You know, between all your book tours and cooking classes."

He smirked and stepped back. He leaned against the counter. "Very funny. What happened after the asshole?"

Thank God he didn't press for details. "I came back

home, licked my wounds, and decided to save money for a European backpacking trip. Until I found out how expensive that was, instead, I enrolled in classes over in Greenville, and next year I'll be the proud owner of a bachelor's degree in communications."

He nodded a few times. "In between all that, you read mystery books."

She grinned. "I do."

He scanned her from her canvas sneakers up to her curly hair. "Cute bookworm."

Her face grew warm, and her stomach flip-flopped. Damn, he had a way of lighting her up inside.

Somewhere in her mind, she couldn't help but wonder if he was disguising himself too. Was he an asshole like Vance, trying to throw her off his real scent? Dazzle her with mystery and intrigue, hook her in like a fish, only to yank her out of the water to reveal a monster.

No, she couldn't think like that. Doubting everyone, because of one prick. Stuff like that didn't happen in this tiny town anyway. Besides, Guy had kindness in his eyes. Something settling, comforting.

Before she could ask him about it, the front door jingled with Ralph's entrance.

"Good, you're both here already. Help me unload the potatoes from my car." He went back outside to open the trunk.

Skye shook her head and called after him. "Would saying please burn your tongue? Or do you think you're charming enough without manners?"

Guy chuckled and held open the door for Skye. The trio carried in multiple bags of spuds, Guy heaving several over his shoulder while she let them dangle at her sides.

"We've got a busy week ahead," Ralph continued,

dropping the bags by the storage closet behind the kitchen. "It's the beginning of flounder season, and I'm expecting Rufus to deliver a bunch today. I've paid extra for the pre-prepped filets, so our new cook doesn't have to de-bone them himself. You're costing me money, Guy."

"I'll make it worth every penny," he replied. He dropped the bags on top of the others and grabbed the other ones from Skye, so she didn't have to take them farther.

"Thank you. It's also the Apple Picking Festival on Saturday." Skye brushed the hair from her face. "Are you going?"

"What's the Apple Picking Festival?"

Ralph rolled his eyes. "A lot of work and plenty of tight-fisted customers." He retreated to his office.

"This place will be packed from sunup through closing," Skye added. "With a wait around lunchtime. We make a special apple cider kicking off with the festival. Then people head out to the apple orchards and pick however many bushels they can carry. Down the main street in town, there are booths with people selling their homemade apple butter, jellies, and pies. Obviously, craft brews and hard ciders flow freely. Not to mention the annual apple pie eating contest. Ralph won second place last year, behind Tommy Krantz."

"That dirtbag cheated," Ralph chimed in from around the corner. "He grabbed the smallest pie."

Skye rolled her eyes. "Not that he's bitter. Anyhoo, just typical small-town festival stuff. Bands playing, games and rides for kids, bobbing for apples of course, and enough funnel cake to send everyone into diabetic comas."

"Sounds delicious." He opened several bags and started placing a bunch in the electric peeler.

"It's the social event of the year. Anyone who's anyone

will be there." Skye jumped up and sat on the counter beside him, making sure the potatoes didn't get stuck in the loader. "Care to mingle with the suspects, Mr. Secret Agent?"

Damn, the way Skye sat on the counter right beside him pulled her skirt up ever so slightly and revealed a little more thigh. Just teasing him. Almost begging him to stare, to wait for more skin, had him aching.

Not that Reed was the ogling type, and it definitely wasn't a good idea to make friends with anyone at this turbulent time in his life. But there was nothing wrong with a little subtle appreciation for this angelic fireball. Innocent enough in her position helping him with the potatoes, he couldn't help appreciate *all* of her.

His reply was cut off by the door jingling with their first customer.

Skye jumped down and rushed to the front. "Good morning, Joan, Margaret." Her jovial voice was a little high. "Is today the day you'll share your secret peach cobbler recipe?"

Reed went back to work, trying like hell to focus. He cast furtive glances in Skye's direction more often than he intended. She was so lively, so animated with everyone. It was impossible not to like her. To be drawn to her like a bear to a honey trap.

A steady stream of customers poured in for the next hour, and he cooked up more than a few dozen scrambled eggs and flipped pound after pound of pancakes. All the potatoes came in handy for the extra hash browns. Only right before the lunch rush did Skye take a break in the kitchen, bringing him another coffee and bottled water.

"Rough weekend?" she asked. A tinge of pink graced her cheeks.

He shoved a tray full of shepherd's pies into the oven. "Why do you ask?"

"Your cap is on backward. I've noticed you wear it that way when you act like a sourpuss."

He chuckled. "Me? A sourpuss?" He shrugged it off because Lord knew he couldn't dare say a word about the frickin' obstacles he ran into trying to break into Joe's account the previous evenings. One step forward, two steps back.

"Tell me about this asshole boyfriend," he dared to press as he pulled out clean plates from the dishwasher. "The one that burned you."

Her sigh was heavy, and her gaze suddenly tired. " Why do you want to break open that hornet's nest?" she asked, sitting on a stool. Her skin glistened with a little sweat from the rush of the day. She sipped on her own bottled water. "You gonna go arrest him, Mr. Six-shooter? And don't think for one second I didn't notice the subject change."

He held up a kitchen knife to start chopping vegetables. "If he hurt you, I could go all *Fried Green Tomatoes* on him."

She scoffed. "Enticing as that idea may be, the food would taste awful. I don't want to risk purging the customers."

He chuckled and kept working. Reed usually didn't get close to civilians, but what could it hurt here? If things suddenly got dicey, he could leave at the drop of a few shell casings. He'd done it before. It wasn't like he and Skye were in any kind of relationship. Hell, he only worked with the woman, nothing more. He had no interest in any entanglements, except maybe of a sexual nature. If she was interested, he wouldn't rule that out. But aside from working together, there'd be nothing past casual encounters. Nothing even remotely permanent. So, getting to know a little more about Skye's personal life was nothing more than passing the time and blending in with his surroundings, because that's what civilians did. Enjoying his brief time here wouldn't hurt anything, right?

At least that's how he rationalized this new diversion. Something enjoyable to help pass the time. Make him feel like a human being. For however little time he had left there.

He let the silence drag on between them as he sharpened the knife, waiting for her to continue. Because he knew she would. It was one of the many tactics he'd learned over the years: eventually, people will fill awkward silences. Especially Skye. She was good at that. Probably what made her a great waitress.

"I wanted to live an urban life in college," she started, throwing him a rag to wipe off the knife. "The big city lights, the noise, atmosphere, all of it. Education was the best way out of here, and I was lucky enough to get a scholarship that took care of the tuition. The first day, I was moving into my dorm, and Vance was there. Helping a friend move into their room. Wow, we hit it off. He was charming, knew everyone, had connections to all the best places—lots of dorm parties, dates downtown, even picnics in the park. The full-court press, as they say, which turned into late nights, and a few missed classes. My grades started to slip."

Reed kept his face straightforward as he continued to chop carrots, garlic, and tomatoes, not wanting to assume anything.

"When I received my first D on a test, I pushed hard into my studies to make up for that—"

"Which meant you didn't spend as much time with him," he filled in that blank easily. He could guess where this trainwreck was headed. He swept the diced vegetables into a pan. The sizzle filled the air with fresh garlic that made his mouth water.

"Yep." Skye grabbed a spatula and stirred it for him while he set the cutting board in the sink. "I didn't see it then, but his possessive side turned dominant. He got really angry when he bought tickets for a concert, and I had to skip it to study for finals. It was the night before my hardest class; I couldn't go. He yelled at me. Grabbed my arm and left a nasty bruise. He apologized so much after that. Filled my room with flowers the next day, even took me to a really fancy dinner after I'd gotten a C on that exam. Then it was just more anger after that point. He always wanted to know where I was every second, including waiting outside some of my classes. Got a little..."

"Creepy?" He took the spatula and continued stirring.

"To say the least. But a tiny part of my brain kept saying it was because he was just that into me. He had a lot of passion for the things he cared for. But then he didn't like me being out with my friends. People I'd known longer than him. He said he didn't trust them, thought they would try and steal me away from him. To this day, I have no idea why he thought that."

Reed tried hard not to let the obvious show on his face. *Because the bastard was a controlling psychopath.* Insecure about themselves, and believed that a show of force was the only way to exert control. He'd seen a lot of them in the cartel. Skye hadn't even finished her story yet, and he knew where it was going. But he bit his tongue. It was important for him to be patient and kind. Real men never needed to use force for control. Control was nothing more than an illusion anyway. He looked at Skye, waiting for her to keep going.

She resumed her seat on the stool. "Looking back, I can

see it coming. I had a group research project for my environmental sciences class. A nice guy in my group, Lloyd...funny too." She smiled. Then it vanished. "Needless to say, Vance didn't like it. Didn't like *him*. He must have spied on our group at the library. When I got back to my dorm room, he was waiting. He'd destroyed my laptop, along with most of my school papers. He'd thrown a bunch of my things down the stairwell." A long moment passed before she continued. "When I went to pick them up, he shoved me down the stairs."

Reed inhaled sharply. His knuckles whitened around the spatula's handle. He slowly set it down, then leaned against the counter. He crossed his arms to hide his fists. Any man who dared hurt a woman, let alone *this* woman, deserved to be tied to a concrete block and dropped in the ocean. Or some other violent, torturous means to an end, something of which Reed had seen many times from the cartel. He knew of a hundred different ways to make a man disappear. Himself included.

"Some really bad bruises, including a pulled muscle in my back, but thank God I didn't break anything."

"Like your neck."

She raised a single eyebrow at him. She downed the rest of her water. "After I got back from the emergency room, he had a brand new laptop waiting on my desk. With a huge vase of roses."

Please tell me you didn't fall for that.

"I tried to break up with him right there. He said, 'You can't leave. I won't let you.'"

Reed's teeth ground together. "What happened then?"

"I left. Dropped out of school completely. Came back here. Which broke my heart, because I knew an education would be my ticket out of here. But I needed my family." She shrugged her shoulder. "Anyway, I got better. Thanks to my best friend, Lynée, she urged me to take a few self-defense classes and enroll at the local community college. And at least I don't have to see Vance's face again."

On a long sigh, he grabbed the spatula and finished stirring. "Any charges filed against asshole-man?"

Skye chunked her empty water bottle in the recycle bin. "Nope. Not when he's the Assistant D.A.'s son."

Shit. Reed shook his head and scraped the cooked vegetables into a casserole dish.

The door jingled with more customers, signaling the start of the lunch rush. Skye stood and adjusted her uniform.

Before she disappeared into the dining area, Reed called her back.

She stopped.

"I'd love to mingle with you at this apple festival. We can plot ways to make douchebags like Vance disappear."

She smiled. "Well, as a secret agent, I'll let you figure that out. I'll just eat some apple pie and be your alibi." With a wink, she went back to work.

CHAPTER 7

AN ENTIRE WEEK of afternoons spent in an old wooden kitchen chair searching Joe's old computer files strained Reed's back nearly to the point of a herniated disc. Even sitting on a pillow didn't alleviate the discomfort. How he missed his comfortable ergonomic chair with extra padding that molded to his ass. He'd been so spoiled early in his career with little luxuries like that, as well as state-of-the-art screens that were easier on the eyes. Not this old laptop that barely had enough RAM and storage to do the job.

But at least now, he was grateful for a decent signal and the proper proxy server to disguise his location. He didn't have to trek all the way out to Seattle nearly as often. Thanks to the additional funds he'd earned at the diner, he now had the means to purchase additional equipment. The remaining funds in his bailout bag had dwindled to precariously low levels.

Of course, things would've gone faster if he hadn't had to run off to his day job in the mornings. But he needed to earn a living somehow. And of course, seeing Skye at the diner made it well worth it.

The clock neared twelve a.m. as Reed's eyes drooped from the weight of the day. The lines started to blur on the screen, and when he shut his eyes, the image of the coding scan had been burned into the back of his eyeballs. He was desperate to find a way into Joe's account with this Dark Inferno game. He was sure that was the key. They'd been his partner's dying words; it had to be important.

Reed jerked himself awake, slapping his cheeks to keep from falling asleep at the desk. He stretched his back and grabbed his empty coffee mug to start another pot of coffee.

As it brewed, he checked all the outdoor cameras again. All his counter measures were still in place should anyone come for him in the dead of night.

The scrolling screen was a jumble of file names and scripts, the numbers blurry. Somehow, between all the endless lines of code, a single file named caught his attention: Fire. He clicked on it.

A notation made by Joe only a few weeks before his death was a simple string of random numbers and letters. Underneath that was a name: *Gigaslave.*

Reed smiled at the obvious jab. Totally just like Joe.

If you're up there, buddy, help me out here.

Reed switched over to the Dark Inferno internet game and plugged in the username and the string of characters. Which he prayed was the password.

The game pulled up, along with all of Joe's player information.

"Yes!" Reed threw his fists into the air and plopped in front of the computer again. This time, he sat on the edge of the chair. This was the farthest he'd gotten in the investigation in months. One dead-end after another, all while trying to stay alive being chased after by ruthless targets. Finally, *he* had something to chase.

The game was brutal. Mercenaries overran cities with demonic brutality, and the goal was for players to form alliances and take back neighborhoods through strategic battles and inventory runs. The impressive graphics left no amount of blood and gore to the imagination.

The in-game chat feature popped up, with a few online players asking where Gigaslave had been. Joe hadn't logged in for a year. Reed ignored them for now.

He scrolled through the previous chat sessions. Tons of them. The last one was the evening before Joe's death.

His breath caught in his throat.

Someone confirming the location of a drop point. All the previous interactions with this player were addresses, times, quantities, and money exchanges. Reed recognized a few of the places, all on the outer edges of El Paso, even out in the desert. The chat went back and back with more than ten drop times over two weeks.

"Shit, he did all of this without telling me?"

His mind whirled with all the new information. Everything his partner had done on his own, without any backup, without uttering a word to Reed. Had Joe gone rogue? Had he been on the take with the very cartel they were assigned to investigate?

The revelation made him sick. All those years working together, side by side, and Reed had never known. Maybe that's why he'd picked Reed as his partner all those years ago because he thought he was expendable. Just another black-hat-criminal kid on whom he could pin all these shady deals.

He swallowed hard, the bitter taste too much to take. "Joe, you son of a bitch, please tell me I'm wrong."

He scrolled through more messages and found one from a contact only a few days before his death.

"Business is good. One mil this time. Don't worry about noise. Slugger has us covered."

One mil. A million-dollar drop. *Shit.* With the number of drops they'd done, there was a history here of over ten million dollars' worth of inventory they were dealing with. That Joe was handling, without his partner.

A ball of lead condensed in Reed's stomach.

This couldn't be true. There had to be something else behind all these exchanges. Whatever plan Joe had, he hadn't seen himself dead at the end of it. Not only that, but there was also no way Joe would ever sell out his partner. Despite what the screen in front of him read, Reed refused to believe it.

Who the hell was Slugger? Cartels often used *noise* as code for law enforcement, or some other rival gang trying to interfere. Whoever Slugger was, he was definitely key. Maybe that was the guy who'd killed Joe. Perhaps he'd found out that Joe was DEA.

Through searching the rest of the chat sessions, there was no other mention of a Slugger. Reed switched over to Joe's offline files and found only one entry as well, on a deleted document titled *Christmas List.*

"Suspect referenced 'Slugger.' New lead."

Reed scrolled up to the top of the file and continued to read.

September 13: New drop point from game chat. 10k exchanged. First contact 'Cesar,' Hispanic male, 30-35 years, 200lbs, thick Northern Mexican accent, relatively uneducated in dialect. Report filed to enter new point of contact. Partner set up our new safe house.

September 18: Second drop this week where suspect didn't show. Waited more than three hours. Chat sessions with perps growing more suspicious and cautious. Checked in with my partner remotely, reportedly focusing on cartel digital footprint to find another lead.

September 24: Successful drop tonight. Over 600k. New suspect in car with first contact. Hispanic male, lighter skin, brown eyes, 20-25 years, 140lbs, formal Spanish. Spoke English fluently no accent. Possibly US citizen. No name given. Talked about next drop in a few days. Nothing firm. Seemed more focused on what I thought about the game. Report filed to enter new point of contact.

October 2: First contact referenced an 'inside man' protecting them from law enforcement. New contact shut him up with a gut punch. Did not specify which law enforcement, Federale, US Border & Customs, or DEA. No name given. Didn't give a new drop point/time. Said they'd see me on the game. Report filed.

October 9: My previous reports on internal systems have disappeared. Intel is missing. Concerned someone inside DEA is tampering with investigation. Could be the 'inside man' they referenced before. Did not file report in case the system is compromised. Will watch my partner more closely since he's the closest one with access to my files. I'm staying at a secondary safehouse for his safety and my confidentiality. Do not suspect he knows of my location.

October 12: Suspect referenced 'Slugger.' New lead. May be 'inside man.' Setup test to rule out my partner as mole. Nothing back yet.

October 15: Drop scheduled 24:00 at new location, El Paso warehouse on Doniphan Drive. Chatter on game quiet. Texting partner the drop location.

The report ended there.

Sitting there reading Joe's last report hit him like a tidal wave. This was the last thing his partner had written. What had been going through his mind? Had he been scared? Did he have regrets about leaving Reed out of all this? He must've known how dangerous it was, having texted for backup. He could imagine the man reloading his weapons for this last drop, looking at his bulletproof vest in his closet and wondering if he should use it.

He should've. Granted, it would've given away his law enforcement status, but he'd be alive. If only Reed had gotten to that warehouse sooner. Maybe they could've arrested those thugs, and Joe could've explained everything implied in this report.

But Reed was too late. Everything had gone south. He'd arrived just in time to see his partner shot in the chest.

He read through the last few entries again, anger climbing like a mushroom cloud. His partner had done all of this in the dark because he thought Reed was a mole. Because he didn't know who to trust.

Shit. How could he think that of me?

The rage pulsed through his chest, too much. He grabbed the coffee mug off the table and pitched it against the wall. The ceramic shattered, leaving a small dent in the panel.

Joe thought I was deleting files.

Reed scraped his hands down the sides of his face. If his partner's reports really were missing from internal systems, that meant there *was* an insider tampering with evidence. Only high-level personnel had access to that. Way above his pay grade. It was possible this "Slugger" had something to do with it. But since Reed was the only one to see these files, that meant the mole was still in the DEA.

The whole world practically shifted on that realization. He stood quickly and backed away from the table. Distancing himself from that knowledge because he didn't want it. The very thought of that made his stomach heave over. And then solidify into molten lead.

Whoever this mole was, they were directly responsible for his partner's death. And for Reed's forced vigilante role. The reason why he couldn't stay in the same place for very long. And why no one had come to back them up after everything happened.

They already suspected that Reed was the mole.

The very idea of him turning on his fellow agents, on his own country, made his blood boil. He loved his job. He'd spent his career using his tech skills to serve his country the best he could. Now he was being inadvertently framed for something that his partner had caught. Likely had suspected Reed all along, since he had a separate apartment.

He scraped his ballcap off his head, scratching at his scalp. Pacing around the kitchen behind the table where he'd worked didn't help clear the fog. He interlaced his fingers behind his head.

Dammit, how he wished he could talk to someone about this. Joe had been an excellent listener, and they'd bounced ideas off each other like real brothers. At least up until the time where he'd closed himself off because he questioned if Reed was a liar.

This was the most progress in the case he'd made in a year, only to have that excitement dashed aside as quickly as it'd come.

God, he really needed to talk to someone.

Reed closed his eyes and tried to process.

The first image in his mind was Skye. Her brilliant blue eyes, that infectious smile that made him want to agree to anything she asked. The urge to grab his phone and call her was so overwhelming. As much as he desperately wanted to tell her everything, he couldn't. There was no way he could explain this setup in the tiny backwoods cabin. Inviting her over was out of the question. Oh yeah, and it was also one in the morning.

A chat bubble popped up on the screen. One he couldn't ignore.

Who the hell are you?

Reed didn't respond. He just continued to stare at the screen. Some guy with the username *LocoLobo.*

An avatar approached his own character. A darkly clad mercenary with weapons in a half dozen holsters and a stealth helmet painted like a wolf. The graphics displayed amazingly detailed glowing yellow eyes and white teeth bared in a growl. He gripped the barrel of a sawed-off shotgun, pointed down at the cracked-soil ground.

I know you're not Gigaslave. Why did you break into his account? The text read in the chat bubble.

Reed's heart pounded hard, the echo loud in his ears to the point where that's all he heard. Not the ding of the screen or the soft hum of the computer fan. How the hell did this guy know? If he was a hacker, there was no way he could see his location. Reed sat in the chair again, slipped his ballcap back on, backward, and dared to type out a response.

What makes you think it's not me?

Several minutes passed before the screen dinged with another message.

Follow me.

The character moved to a crumbling building in the background. A dilapidated barn with the door hanging open.

Using his keyboard, he made Joe's avatar follow slowly, though he was certain this was a trap. But he had to know. This guy knew something.

Inside the barn, the wolf avatar stood beside a pillar in the center of the space. Only it was no longer a barn. It had become a warehouse. Dusty, empty concrete with a single pallet in the middle stacked with boxes.

The wolf face sneered at him.

The chat bubble returned. *Does this look familiar?*

A foot jutted out from behind the box.

Reed moved his character around the pallet stack to see a form laying on the ground.

Another character that looked a little like the digitized form of...

He gasped.

Joe.

With three bullets in his chest.

The exact way his partner had died in real life.

His blood crystallized in his veins.

The screen dinged with another message. *I made this special for you. DEA.*

"You son of a bitch," Reed whispered at the screen.

LocoLobo was Joe's killer. No one else had seen his partner die except the man on the other end of the gun. The game designer was Joe's murderer. That was his target.

Now everyone can relive this moment. And he can die countless times in high definition.

Reed's fingers curled around the mouse threatening it to break. He made his character pull his gun and fire a shot into LocoLobo's snarling face. The bullet screamed toward the mask until it dissolved into a spray of fire sparks, leaving the wolf unharmed.

The screen dinged again. *Enjoy the game, gringo. I'll find you soon enough.*

The character vanished.

He stood from the chair, his breathing fast and angry.

He'd found him. The bastard who'd ruined his life.

The jackass's threat might've scared the crap out of anyone else. But not Reed. That bolstered his resolve. No one could find him. He was one of the best at cybersecurity, and not many in the world could locate him with the proxies he had in place and all his masking efforts. He was considered an expert hacker by the time he was sixteen. But a little part of him wanted this bastard to find him. So Reed could empty a clip into his chest.

He resumed his seat, and couldn't help but let the corner of his mouth lift. He now had another lead. One that gave him a much more distinct direction to head toward—one a techy like him relished.

LocoLobo had put a target on his own digital back. It was only a matter of time before Reed found *him*.

Diego smiled at his laptop, resting on his lap. Then downed the rest of his tequila in a tall shot glass. The back patio was his favorite part of his small hacienda. The perfect view of the hills in the distance showcased a lake at the bottom that glimmered in the moonlight. Another reason he loved this place so much was that it was on the other side of town, outside the cartel's compound. A specific choice he made that his uncle had agreed to, just in case the compound was ever raided by the army.

More importantly, it gave Diego the freedom to do his digital dirty work in peace. Without a boss looking over his shoulder and hounding him on deadlines, ratings, and fucking timecards. He'd done that during his internship in college in the States. He never wanted to do that again. He much preferred his current endeavors.

Sitting here in the warm evening, uncovering slimy

DEA scum, and making them shit their pants on the other side of a screen is what he loved. Because he was certain that's what this other idiot was doing. Stuck in a DEA cubicle somewhere, going over the files of the agent he'd killed, searching for more clues. *Took those suckers long enough.*

If he was lucky, Diego might've been talking to the other agent he'd been searching for this whole time. Something in his gut told him that's who was on the other side of the chat bubble. He'd created the new barn scene depicting the real-life scenario of the DEA agent's death, just to fuck with the guy. To distract him, enrage him enough to make a mistake and reveal his location. Diego's software was already hard at work identifying the man's IP address and location. In only a small matter of time, he'd know for certain who this was, and where to go knocking down his door.

That beautiful moment of his first law-enforcement kill was now preserved in this digital game for all time. His baby—Dark Inferno—replaying the glorious gunshots over and over for hundreds of thousands of players around the world. Reveling in the joy of that *cabron's* exquisitely detailed death.

He shut his laptop, refilled his shot glass from the tequila bottle on the table, and sipped the contents. Basking in his achievement. Tomorrow he'd send assassins to Wherever, USA, to rid the world of this DEA nuisance for good. Then prove he was fully capable of taking his uncle's place in every way.

CHAPTER 8

"READY, MR. MAN-on-the-Run?"

Reed glanced up to his new enchantment in her pale pink short-sleeve sweater, snug blue jeans, and black boots. She looked just as delectable as she had that morning for their shift. But now the diner was closed, he was finishing the side duties while she'd run home to spruce up for their first date. If that's what they were going to call it.

He pushed the stainless steel bowls back on the shelf and stood.

"Ready for what?" He feigned confusion, pretending to look through cabinets.

Her eyes rounded. "The apple festival."

"Oh, that's today?"

She smacked his upper arm. "Your memory is much better than that. Now, do you want to change clothes or not? Either way, I don't care."

"Yeah, I should probably change."

He couldn't resist playing with her. He slipped off his cap and apron, laying them on the prep counter, then he whipped off his T-shirt.

Her eyes went as big as their pancake platter.

Just the reaction he wanted. When he went for the button on his pants, her hand flew up.

"Wait! Don't change here. The diner may be closed, but...go to the bathroom or breakroom." Her cheeks flushed, the color brighter than her sweater.

She was so flippin' adorable. He hadn't had this much fun in years.

He chuckled. "Didn't take you for the shy type." He gathered his stuff and went to the backroom to put on a clean T-shirt. His knife was still safely tucked in his ankle sheath.

After a few minutes, they both piled into his truck, and she directed them to the best place to park at the festival. Whatever kind of outing Skye called this, Reed really needed this date. Something to fill his brain with the lighter side of life. Things had become far too intense in his little cabin with the recent revelations. Every time he walked into the place, his computer equipment stared at him, mocking him for not having found Joe's killer yet. After the other night in the game, Reed had worked tirelessly to find his address, tracing his IP and any other digital trail he'd left. To no avail. The man was extremely gifted in covering his tracks.

Reed would find him. Eventually. It would just take time and patience. And a fresh afternoon out with Skye to remind him he was still human.

White tents and pedestrians filled Main Street with barely any pavement visible anymore. Reed had to be extra cautious despite the joyous atmosphere. Crowded events like this were great places for perps to hide.

"I like to start at this end and head north," she pointed up the street, oblivious to his sudden hesitant frame-of-mind. "My first stop is always Maybelle's jams and jellies. Best in town."

After some *how you dos* with several locals and

frequent diner customers, Skye took his hand and led him to the next booth. Her delicate fingers wrapped around his and sent a warmth up his arm. Just the simple, casual touch subtly relaxed him. He couldn't remember the last time he held a woman's hand.

Too damn long, that's when.

"Hi, SueAnne."

"Hi, Skye. How's my favorite patron?" A tall, somewhat-older Native American woman pulled reading glasses off her face and let them dangle on a chain around her neck.

"Great. This is Guy, the diner's new cook."

SueAnne stuck out her hand and offered a gracious smile. Then spoke a few words in her Native American dialect.

He assumed it meant *nice to meet you.*

"You too," he replied.

Skye lifted a candle in a glass Mason jar to his nose. "Take a whiff."

Something fruity mixed in with the unmistakable apple smell. Not bad. He wasn't much of a candle-guy. Maybe when the electricity went out, but not for making a place overburdened with a flavored waxy smell.

"Her crab apple scent is my favorite. And this one," she lifted a dark red jar to his nose. He picked up a spicy note. "This one's cinnamon apple."

"Nice."

"Aren't they? SueAnne has made soy candles for these festivals for years. Oh, look!" Her eyes lit up, and she moved to the other side of a table. "You've added soaps this year."

"Yes," the lady followed her. "One of our tribal leaders needed an organic soap for his skin. I made these to help him. He loved them so much, I made a huge batch."

"They smell divine. Like lavender and honeysuckle." She held out a bar for him to smell.

Reed breathed it in. Clean and feminine.

Yeah, that would smell amazing on her.

Way too quickly, images of Skye in the shower lathering herself in the soap flooded his mind. "Yeah, that's..." He had to clear his throat. "That's really nice."

"Please, take a sample. Let me know what you think." SueAnn placed a bar wrapped in twine in a paper bag.

"You are so sweet, thank you." She looked across the candles again.

Reed scanned around him again, pretending to admire the festival's atmosphere. But was really searching for out-of-place strangers. Any hint of the cartel or DEA. He couldn't shake his cautious nature. He'd been burned too many times during times when he thought he could let down his guard. Not to mention clear his mind from the delectable images in his brain inspired by the soap.

"I'll take the cinnamon apple and the raspberry," Skye announced.

"And I'll take the crab apple," Reed added.

Why the hell not? He pulled out his wallet and paid for all three candles.

As SueAnne wrapped the jars in paper, Skye leaned in. "Thanks. You didn't have to do that."

"I'm happy to." He smiled back. He had to admit, having Skye look up at him with that smile damn-near made his day. Made him relax just a touch.

She glanced down at her watch. "Okay, let's make our way to the stage. Ralph is scheduled to compete in the pie-eating contest soon."

This time he took her hand. "Lead the way."

They sat a few rows back from the white, make-shift

stage. He made sure they were on the end, more convenient for a quick getaway if needed. He kept watching people's faces, their hands, anything to cue him they were tailing him. Somehow he managed to keep a calm expression. Reed wasn't expecting any surprises, but one could never be too sure, even tucked away in the foothills of Snoqualmie Mountain.

Skye's fingers flew over her phone.

"What's up?"

"I'm texting my friend, Lynée." A few seconds passed, and she smiled. "Cool. She's gonna meet us after this at the hayrides."

Something tugged on his left sleeve. He looked over at a blondish boy no older than five peering up at him with curious eyes. A gooey caramel-covered apple jutted out from his fist, with the same concoction smeared on his nose, lips, and chin.

His mother seemed occupied on the other side, talking to a friend.

"I'm Bobby," he announced. "What's your name?"

He opened his mouth to answer, but the kid kept on talking. "Mama says I shouldn't talk to strangers, but I think you're okay. I like Miss Skye. She trusts you. Right?"

It was hard not to chuckle. "Well, your mama's right. You shouldn't talk to strangers. But I like Miss Skye, too. What do you like most about her?"

"She brings me pancakes at the diner with extra syrup. And my ice cream has chocolate sprinkles in a smiley face."

Now, he did chuckle. "That sounds delicious. How's that caramel apple?"

His eyes lit up. "Sticky."

"Bobby, don't bother the nice man." His mother finally leaned over. She gave an apologetic smile. "He didn't get anything on you, did he?"

"No, he's fine," Reed replied, then looked back at Bobby. "It was nice talking to you. Enjoy the contest."

The kid went back to devouring his apple.

Skye had paused in her texts to watch him. Her expression was sweet, that adorable dimple showing up on one of her cheeks.

"What?" he asked.

A round man with wide-set eyes and thin lips took the stage and spoke into a mic. "Afternoon, everyone."

Skye leaned close. "That's Mayor Stubblefield."

"I hope you all are enjoying the ninety-first year of Cascade Creek's Apple Picking Festival," the mayor began. "This county is a proud grower of three-percent of the nation's apples..."

"Wow," Reed said under his breath.

"And this year's festival proceeds go to the Boys and Girls Club of Kittitas County." The mayor outstretched a hand to the right as a bunch of kids and adults in blue shirts waved to the crowd.

"Without further *ado*, let's get to the main event everyone looks forward to the most. I hope you all brought your appetites." The mayor introduced the contestants and covered the rules.

"Ralph upped his training this year to beat Tommy." Skye tended close again.

He was nearly distracted by her scent. He couldn't tell if it was perfume or her shampoo, but the flowery sweetness was so becoming on her. Very fitting. "Oh?"

"Notice him drinking lots of water and chewing lots of gum?"

Reed had noticed that but didn't think too much of it. He nodded.

"Well, he claims that's all part of his training."

The horn sounded to start the contest. The crowd went wild, calling out names and cheering on their favorite contestants. Tommy and Ralph seemed to be the favorites.

With their hands clutched behind their backs, the men dove face-first into their apple pies. Reed watched as they all gobbled large chunks at a time, steadily devouring the pie from the pan. It was going to be close.

Then Ralph jumped up, hands high in the air, and pie smeared over his face. The horn sounded. Tommy lifted his head and frowned.

The mayor inspected Ralph's pan. "This year's champion is Ralph Summerlin," the mayor announced, holding his hand up in victory. "He's won the coveted Apple Trophy, as well as bragging rights until next year."

Reed was fairly sure that was the first time he'd seen the man smile.

The crowd cheered and applauded. Skye put two fingers in her mouth and let out a loud, long whistle.

Damn! What other fascinating things could she do with that mouth?

She laughed, and a pink blush graced her cheeks.

"Who'da thought Ralph was the competitive type?" Reed chuckled.

"Oh, you don't know the half of it. When he loses, boy, can he hold a grudge. But since he won this contest, life will be a lot easier at the diner for a few weeks." She laughed. "They have another contest with the kids, so let's go get in line for the hayrides."

"Onward, fearless leader."

Again, she grabbed his hand, and they walked up the street several blocks.

"You like leading me around, don't you?"

"Maybe." She grinned. "Get used to it. We're out here tomorrow at nine a.m. when the orchards open."

What? "Tomorrow?" So no trips to Seattle for research.

"Yup. This is a two-day event. Frankly, it's the biggest one in Cascade Creek. It's grown over the years. It pulls people from Greenville, Florence, really all the surrounding counties."

Skye talked about wanting to get out of this town, but the pride in her voice contradicted her. She was a walking paradox that kept him guessing every day. Maybe it wasn't necessarily the small-town life she resented, only the lack of excitement. A desire for something new. Different. Lord knew much of his career was spent doing the same, mundane routine every day. But he could see how waiting tables to the same customers, the same meals, day in and day out for years would drive him crazy. But she loved her friends. She loved guiding him around and showing him her world, introducing something new. Just from the look on her face, all lit up with energy, that was obvious.

They made it to the line for hayrides. Skye bopped on her tiptoes, her head darting this way and that, then she pulled her cell phone out of her back pocket. Likely texting Lynée.

He swallowed a chuckle. He could just imagine texting Joe:

I'm carrying scented candles and waiting for a hayride. Are you coming?

His former partner would've probably laughed his ass off. Making Reed the target of his jokes for the next month.

Fuck! He missed that man. Brothers couldn't be closer. There wasn't a day that went by that he didn't think about Joe or his antics or the way he could drill down any situation into its barest form. Reed even missed this constant ribbing on his technology infatuation.

"Hey. Where'd you go?" Skye's sweet pink lips frowned at him.

"Just wondering how long this line will take?"

"Oh, it shouldn't be too long. They have three trailers. Besides, Lynée and her cousin are coming."

"Hi, guys."

Reed turned to see a strawberry blonde, about Skye's height, and a shorter brunette smiling at them.

"Hi." Skye's voice went up an octave as she hugged the women.

"Guy, this is Lynée and Josie."

"Nice to meet you, ladies." Reed watched their hands full of bags from treasured purchases.

"So, you're the illustrious new chef in town." Lynée smiled.

Skye could hardly contain her glee with Guy on her arm. The appreciation all over her friends' faces with just one look at him made her even giddier. What a concept, to be proud of her date, and he not be overly protective and controlling. Comfortable in his own skin. His toned muscles packed into his gray T-shirt, his deep brown eyes that seemed to take in everything, or his bite-worthy ass that made you want to grab a hold with both hands—the whole enchilada.

"So, how's the job goin'?" Lynée asked.

"Haven't killed anyone yet, so that's a good sign."

The women chuckled. Skye smiled. After waiting a few minutes, their tractor pulled up. With a helping hand from Guy, the ladies climbed onto the flatbed and took a seat on the bales of hay.

"This will take us past Gordon's orchards and around Rimmer's olive farm. There are some great views of the pass. Have you ever skied up here before, Guy?"

"Can't say I have."

"What's the likelihood of Skye turning you into a permanent mountain man?" Lynée dared to ask. "Or are you here just hiding out for the winter?"

Any amusement on Reed's face disappeared.

Skye nudged her with an elbow and a not-so-subtle glare.

An awkward silence stretched between the group. Like jagged nails dragged along her back.

"He already told me." Skye smiled, trying to lighten the sudden dark mood. "He's a secret agent looking for his next target. The perfect clam chowder recipe. He plans on stealing the diner's version and claiming it for his own."

He scoffed, and his smile returned. "Who knew the world's most dangerous dish was in sleepy Cascade Creek? Gotta save the world somehow."

"One spoonful at a time." Lynée giggled.

The tractor went over a few potholes in the dirt road leading to Gordon's. "Hang on," the driver called.

Skye bounced in her seat. Before she could get a firm sitting, they hit another pothole. She flew up from her perch and pitched forward. Guy reached out, grabbed her waist, and pulled her back onto the hay bale before she crashed to the floor.

Her heart skipped as she clutched the hay. Guy's grip was firm and sure on her body. "Fast hands. Thanks for that."

"Don't mention it." The corners of his perfect mouth curved upward, and she admitted those were some incredibly tempting lips.

She turned her head to hide the blush she was sure crept over her cheeks.

"Too much rain," Josie said with a frown. "It makes these roads like swiss cheese."

To her delight, Guy kept a hand wrapped around her waist for the rest of the jarring trip.

When they finally stopped, he jumped down first, then held out his hand to all the ladies. Skye was last. He lifted her by the waist, as if she weighed no more than a plate of her own apple pie, and set her down on the ground. The contact made her melt a little more inside. She didn't want him to let go.

"Sorry about Lynée," she whispered in his ear. "She can be a bit direct when she turns protective."

Guy rubbed the small of her back in small circles, so soothing. "Protective friends are a good thing. And I've had much worse inquisitions."

Bits of straw and hay covered Guy's pants and his back. She started swiping off a few from his shirt. Her hand hit something hard, probably his belt. He turned just as she swiped once more, and her hand brushed across his crutch a little rough. A complete accident and she bit her lip.

"Sorry."

He laughed and swiped off the rest. His blush made her cringe inside.

"What's the plan, guys?" Josie asked after she replaced her sunhat.

"Does this event have beer?" Guy winked at her.

The sun glinted off his eyes in a brilliant amber, and his rugged face looked tanner than before.

Lynée gave Skye a look.

"Follow me, Mr. BB Gun. We have the best hard cider in the entire state." Skye knew it. The man deserved a beer after the last ride. And her accidental groping.

They arrived at a tent full of various flavored hard ciders, and she ordered four large glasses. "Thanks, Parker." The owner waved at her from the other side, helping a few other patrons. She handed one to Guy. "Give this a try."

He took one from her hand, his amber gaze glued to her face. Even during his first large gulp, he never looked away. He wiped the excess that dribbled from his chin. "Not bad."

"Take it easy. This stuff goes straight to your head," Lynée said. "By the way, I'd like to find something for my mom, since she couldn't make it out this year."

"And I want to buy a wind chime for my sister," Josie added.

"Sounds good. Then we can go to Rooster's for dinner." As they meandered down Main Street, Lynée and Josie strolling several paces ahead, Skye glanced up at Guy. He really seemed to take in the surroundings, absorb the atmosphere. What she found most interesting about him was that he seemed to like watching people. Like he'd never been to a festival before. Everywhere they went, his head never stopped scanning. "Has this town grown on you?"

He took a second before he answered. "Surprisingly so. Especially a few people."

"We might make a small-town mountain man out of you yet."

"Doesn't that require me to grow a three-foot-long beard and wear bearskins?"

"If you like."

"Could you get used to that look on me?"

She slipped her hand in his, entwining their fingers together. The simple gesture had her heart skipping a beat until he tightened his hold and pulled her in closer. Her body fit perfectly into his side. Her heart thumped wildly. Sure, it could've been the cider or all the extra fresh air. But Skye liked the idea of having a sexy man on her arm. With eyes only for her.

I could get used to this.

Wow. How long had it been since Reed held a woman's hand? Or strolled down a street seemingly without a care in the world? When she started cleaning off his shirt and hit the butt of his pistol ducked in his back waistband, he'd panicked and tried to cover it. Only to end up fondled in the process. Which honestly, he didn't mind. He was more concerned about her finding his *other* gun.

But that was just the moment he realized how badly his member needed attention. It had been far too long since his last release, he couldn't even remember when. Thank God the cider could help cool him off.

Old habits kept him searching every face that passed by, watching people's hands, discreetly peering around corners, and monitoring exit points. He had to be on his guard around all these festival-goers in case someone showed up to finish him off. The cider didn't have a chance at dulling those instincts. A gunfight would put an end to this whole fanfare damn quick.

Worst of all, he could be endangering Skye. Just by holding her hand.

But damn, he couldn't stop. She felt so good to hold, drawn to his side. He tucked her hand into the crook of his arm, letting her sweet perfume waft over him. He'd hold onto this memory to keep him sane during dark moments, wherever he ended up.

The idea of leaving this place twisted his stomach. None of the other places he'd hidden out in over the last year impacted him like this. Cascade Creek had given him a reason to stay for once. His spirits dimmed at the prospect of running again.

Think of something else. Quick.

"How's school going?" he asked. The other ladies walked several feet ahead, perusing a few booths as Reed strolled with Skye on his arm.

"Good. Taking my core comm classes now."

"What would you like to do after you graduate?" Keeping up the facade of being an average Joe was vital for an outcast on the run. Still, part of it was also the strong interest in this woman walking beside him. The tractor ride was more than worth it because he got to hold Skye. His only regret was that he couldn't pull her closer. Not without creating a scene.

"I'm not exactly sure. Maybe work in public relations or for a security firm."

"Security?"

"Yeah. Wouldn't that be cool? Surveillance, security, possibly guard dogs. Protecting people from bad guys." Her eyes nearly sparkled with intrigue.

He shouldn't be surprised. Skye would probably be good at security, her imagination would be great for leaving no stone unturned. "I'd feel a little sorry for the criminals if they had to try and hide from you."

She gasped. "Ooh, or maybe the police academy. Do you think I'd make a good cop?"

The face of Joe's murderer flashed in his mind, those evil eyes and vicious face...

The idea of Skye facing that man made his blood boil. His protective instincts kicked in, and it was the last thing in the world he wanted for this incredible woman. After just one week facing the kind of horrors he'd dealt with in his career... her infectious optimism would be snuffed out. Granted, her stellar people-skills and attention to detail would make one kick-ass detective. Why wouldn't she make a great cop?

Check yourself, Reed. He shouldn't doubt her capabilities or partake in a Neanderthal mentality. He'd known some excellent female agents over the years.

Shit, but he couldn't help the thought of her in a chokehold from a perp on meth, or getting shot in a routine traffic stop.

"You don't think I'd make a good police officer?" Her voice lowered.

He looked up to see her dejected expression. "Oh, no. You'd be awesome."

"You paused."

"I'm sorry, I was just thinking of...you and..."

She smirked. "Me up against a bunch of mean criminals, getting thrown to the ground by a brute twice my size?"

He gave her a stunned look. *Did I say all that out loud?*

She chuckled. "Lynée's not the only protective type around here, Guy. It's written all over your face. Sure, the attitude is a bit chauvinistic, but I know it comes from a good place with good intentions."

"Damn, you make me sound like a misogynist." He side-stepped a group of kids running across their path. Lynée and Josie approached a casual restaurant's front patio, looked back at them, and continued whispering.

"Well, knowing is half the battle. Now that you know, how are you going to change the behavior?" She snickered. "Now I sound like Lynée."

The way Skye could read people shamed him at his own job.

"Let me be perfectly clear." He stopped and tugged her in front of him. Holding onto her arms gently.

With just a tilt of her head, her hair fell forward, framing her angelic face. Everything about her was soft.

The sun sank lower behind her just over the treeline, the pink and purple light haloing around her head.

"If you wanted to be a police officer, you'd be incredible at it. Or whatever else you set your mind to."

CHAPTER 9

THE SUN HAD ducked behind a mountain peak by the time they finished dinner. Street lamps glowed in the twilight, and a brilliant canopy of twinkle lights dangled across the main road. Reed followed the women past a few more booths, truly having enjoyed a simple meal without being in a rush to finish. He'd let the trio do most of the talking, and successfully dodged any probing questions directed at him. He'd gotten good at that lately.

Skye had touched his knee under the table a few times, the innocent gesture reassuring and soothing.

This was what ordinary people did on dates. In small towns. No dramatics, no shoot-outs, just simple conversation, and genuine interactions. Man, he craved this.

Following Skye and her friends along the street as they perused more booths felt like the most natural thing in the world. They paused at one, filled with jewelry.

A little farther down, a different one caught his eye. One filled with ornate wood carvings.

"I'm going to check out this one," he told Skye.

She nodded and winked.

The owner greeted him with a smile, and his handlebar mustache twitched. "Hi, I'm Jude. See anything you like?"

"A few." Some of the pocket knives with wooden handles reminded him of something Joe would've loved.

"I carve everything by hand," Jude continued. "On this wall are pictures of commissions I did."

"Nice. How long does it take you to complete one of those?"

"A few weeks." The man was talented—everything from hearts to headboards to Harley-Davidson plaques. A relief wood carving of a lion pulled his attention. The detail in the lion's mane was extraordinary.

Skye's voice made Reed's ear perk up. Not her usual upbeat self. More pinched and harsh. Definitely not like her. He shifted away from the booth to have eyes on her.

She'd turned pale. She stared at someone, though most of her body was turned away from some blond, gel-haired man. Maybe two inches shorter than himself smiled and wrapped a hand around her upper arm.

The pressure rose in Reed's chest, and heat crept up his face.

"It's been a long time, Skye," the face started.

Her eyes lost their sparkle. "Not long enough, Vance. What are you doing here?"

Reed circled around a couple at the booth, making his way to her. So this was the asshole. He was hoping to meet this prick at some point in his life. On a quick glance, Vance didn't have a pistol concealed in his pockets, but that didn't mean he wasn't carrying. Or had some other weapon. Lynée and Josie were several booths down, clearly unaware of what was happening.

"I've been looking for you," Vance cooed, obviously unthwarted by her aversion.

"Have you now?" Reed chimed in, giving an over-exuberant smile. He draped his hand over Skye's shoulders.

"Hi, pumpkin. Who's your friend?"

A glimmer of relief crossed her face. "Guy, this is Vance." She was still far too pale.

"Well, son of a gun." Reed offered his hand. "I've heard a lot about you."

Out of sheer habit, the bastard Vance shook his hand.

Reed gripped hard and didn't let go.

Lynée returned, her smile instantly vanishing when she saw Vance. "What are *you* doing here?" She stood partially in front of Skye as if shielding her.

The man was much taller than both of them. Something he obviously flaunted by trying to step closer to her.

Reed wasn't going to have any of it. He removed his arm from Skye and slapped the man on the back with the facade of a friendly gesture. But really, he was just checking if the prick had a weapon in his waistband. Nothing there. Then he draped his arm across Vance's shoulders, closing around his neck nonchalantly. "Any friend of Skye's is a friend of mine." He gave her a wink and started walking the man up the street and away from the women.

When Vance tried to pull out from under Reed's arm, he didn't let go, which made the shithead's spine stiffen. "So, uh... She's talked about me?"

"Sure. From her description, I recognized you the second I saw you." *At least, your kind, anyway.*

"I must have left an impression." His smug smile came off more sickly.

"Several. I know for a fact Skye has memories of her time with you that feel as fresh as yesterday." Reed tightened his grip around Vance's neck and his hand. Then he dropped his voice, "So if I were you, I would seriously consider leaving these memories in the past. Skye too."

The man cowered under his hold until he was released. Then stiffened with a considerably darker expression.

"Now, you hurry on your way. And do watch out for those steps."

The stairs down the hill leading toward the courthouse were still a good ten yards away, but from Vance's narrowed eyes, he knew *exactly* what Reed referred to.

"Are you threatening me? That would be very stupid. My dad's a lawyer."

Reed let a low chuckle rise up his throat. "I don't threaten, kid. As much as I'd *love* to chat with your dear old dad—and I really would—why not let this friendly conversation stay between us two men." He let the last word hang in the air, staring hard at the prick. Because this guy was not a real man. "Do you get my meaning, pal?"

"I'm not your pal." Shithead somehow found his big boy voice and shucked off Reed's hand. It was impossible for Reed to take his pretty boy scowl seriously. "I don't know what you're implying, but you clearly have no idea what really happened between Skye and me. Why don't you run along before you get hurt?"

Reed shook his head, letting his chuckle grow to an outright laugh. "As entertaining as that may be to watch, you didn't get my meaning. You must be more of a literal guy. So, I'll make this really simple." He took one step forward, which made Vance step back. He held the man's stare. "Come near Skye again, and by the time I'm done with you, even your lawyer-daddy won't be able to recognize you."

Vance stammered. Then he stepped back again, this time reaching the street curb. His heel slipped, and his eyes widened.

Reed reached out and grabbed the man's shoulder. He

held the man over the step, forcefully keeping him there. "Those suckers can be slippery. But then again, you already knew that." He finally pulled him back and let him loose.

Frat boy backed away, casting a suspicious glare at him.

"Say hi to your dad for me, Vance." He smiled.

Shithead shoved his hands in his pockets and retreated to the parking lot.

He better pray I never see his face again.

He spun around and headed straight back to Skye, still stunned, but her color was coming back.

Lynée, the awesome friend she was, stayed beside her the whole time Reed had his confrontation.

"Are you all right?" he asked Skye softly.

"Yes," she replied. Her voice shook.

Her pale face and shaking hands made him so furious inside, it had taken so much of his self-control not to pummel the man where he stood. But that would draw far too much attention with all these people around. Which was the last thing she would've wanted, drawing more attention to herself. Plus, he was secretly trying to keep a low profile.

Damn. The man had really done a number over her. And she'd just had to relive it all without warning. Thank God they were in public. Who knows what that scumbag would've tried to do if others weren't around. Yet, having to face Vance again in front of people probably made her more embarrassed. The last thing he wanted her to feel around him was humiliated.

"Do you want me to take you home?"

Skye stared into Guy's chocolate eyes, still reeling from her interaction with Vance. She forced a deep breath to calm her nerves and bring her back to the here-and-now.

"I'm going to talk to Wyatt," Lynée announced. "The sheriff should know what's going on if that son-of-a-gun decides to show his face around here again."

The mortification continues. After all this time, she still couldn't escape the shit-storm that was Vance. "Oh, please, no, Lynnie. He has much more important things to do right now."

"Domestic violence is not something to sweep under a booth table, Skye. You deserve better. I will *not* allow you to be a statistic." She looked at Guy. "You got her for a minute?"

"Always." His reassuring smile softened her resolve. Lynée trounced off to find the sheriff.

"Thank you," she said. "I...I didn't expect to ever see him again. Especially not here."

Guy gently took her hand in his. "It's all right if you want to cut the evening short."

"No, of course not," she replied quickly. "He will *not* have any control over my decisions ever again. But I think I just need a few seconds." After several deep breaths, her heart rate wouldn't slow down. That familiar fear from her freshman year wrapped around her chest like a vice. She pinched her eyes closed. "Crap, I didn't react well at all, did I? I panicked."

"You handled yourself very well." His smile was small but genuine. His warm hands grounded her back to the moment. The cool breeze, the scent of apples and powdered sugar from the waffle cake stand, and the musical whirring whistles from the kiddie carousel.

"I wouldn't make a very good police officer after all." A tear slipped.

"Shh, you're way too hard on yourself." He wiped her cheek with his sleeve. "But nothing will happen to you as long as I'm around. If you'd like, I can track him down and make him a very good punching bag."

She chuckled through a sniffle.

"It'll be very therapeutic," Guy explained. "He'll have both hands tied behind his back and duct tape over his mouth. And you can just wail on him. Or better yet, why don't we open our own festival booth? Charge money and call it Whack-a-Dick."

Now, she outright laughed. She'd almost pay money to see that herself.

"There's that smile." He held both her hands in his and kissed her knuckles.

Thank God for him. She never expected to be laughing that quickly after seeing her ex.

"I can take you home if you want, but I don't want you left alone tonight."

She contemplated his words—so much meaning behind them. The idea of being alone with Guy made her so warm and fuzzy inside. But she realized she truly meant what she said. Not letting the jerk have any control over her life. She wanted to stay at the festival with Guy. No matter what, she was going to live her life the way *she* wanted. "I don't want to leave. Let's watch the fireworks."

The corner of his lips curled. "I'm game."

Guy held her hand the rest of their stroll, gentle but firm, like a tether keeping her afloat. Twenty minutes before the fireworks started, Lynée spread out the large blanket she'd retrieved from her car, and the ladies took a seat. Guy rounded up some cider for the group.

"Are you *really* okay?" Lynée asked while he was occupied paying for their drinks. Her friend's eyes behind her black-rimmed glasses were full.

"I am. Just shook up."

"Wyatt said he'd drive by your house himself several times tonight and include your address in their rounds throughout the week. All the deputies have Vance's picture, too."

Skye tried to keep from cringing. Lynée meant well, and knowing she had her back through this meant the world. But now Wyatt and all the police around here would see her as a victim. Every time they would come into the diner from this point on, she'd have to suffer through sympathetic looks and constant questions. Another tick in the cons-column of small towns. "Thanks," she finally managed. "But I'd rather if you spent the night at my place tonight, instead? Would that be okay?"

Her friend cupped a hand over her forearm. "Absolutely."

"Smile, you two." Josie held up her phone for a picture.

Guy returned with four tall ciders and sat on the blanket beside her. Amazing how just his presence gave her such relief. Her shoulders relaxed, and her hands stopped shaking.

What would she have done if Guy wasn't around? Granted, they were in a public place, and Vance probably wouldn't have tried anything violent in front of so many people. But he'd gotten away with so much for so long, especially with his daddy as his safety-net. Even if he'd walked away, he wouldn't have truly disappeared for good.

After the interaction with Guy, Skye felt sure Vance was truly gone once and for all. "Thanks again, Guy."

"Anytime." He returned the smile and wrapped an arm around her waist. "Let me know if that festival booth sounds good to you. I'm sure it'll be the most popular."

She swatted at his chest.

Josie snapped a few photos of people around, then

turned to the group. "You both look adorable. Look here and smile."

Skye pulled Guy closer.

Guy held up his hand, blocking his face. "No thanks."

"Aw, come on," Josie replied. "With the twinkle lights behind you, it's so pretty. Just a quick shot."

"Are you shy?" Skye murmured playfully in his ear.

He kept his head turned toward her. "I'm not a fan of photos on social media."

Skye frowned. "Why not?"

Josie kept complaining in the background, clicking away any shot she could with Guy's face.

Guy whispered in Skye's ear. "How do you think Vance found you?"

She bit her lip, the realization hitting her like a pie in the face. Maybe he was right. She plucked Josie's straw hat off the blanket and held it in front of both her and Guy's face, leaning in to make it seem like they were kissing behind it.

Lynée giggled, and Josie whistled as camera flashes lit up the sky around them.

"It's okay," Skye whispered behind the cover of the hat. "Your secret is safe with me."

The corner of Guy's mouth lifted. "What secret?"

"You're afraid the government will find you."

His smile vanished. His brilliant, brandy eyes looked absolutely stunned.

Skye continued. "Because you're a superhero, and they want to conduct top-secret experiments on your DNA to clone you."

Guy let out a breath and chuckled.

How easy it would be to lean in and kiss him right now. Just a quick one. The urge was so strong. For a split second, she thought she saw his eyes trail down her mouth. Maybe he was thinking the same thing.

The music played over the speakers strategically hanging on the lamp posts. She dropped the hat and leaned back on the blanket. Within a few minutes, the fireworks began. Everyone trained their sights on the light show in the sky.

Her mind was trained on Guy. She felt safe with him, close to him. She couldn't say the last time she felt so utterly content in a man's arms.

Was she moving too fast? Wasn't this precisely what got her in trouble with Vance? She'd trusted him and jumped in with both feet without first testing the waters.

She couldn't go through all that again. It was hands-down the worst time of her life. Not just the physical abuse, but the verbal abuse, the manipulation, the over-controlling leash around her heart, and the way he'd made her feel as if everything was her fault. She'd gotten to the point where she was afraid of saying the wrong thing for fear it would set him off.

Her short-lived time with Vance had left an indelible mark. She'd promised herself not to repeat that mistake again. Is that what she was doing with Guy?

No. Guy was nothing like Vance, of that she was sure. But there was nothing wrong with pumping the brakes a bit. Or testing the waters, like she hadn't done with Vance.

She shifted in her seat.

If I kiss him, would it ruin everything?

A little battle played out in her head, timed with the *booms* and *pops*.

Am I infatuated with him because he's a knight in shining armor? Or just because he's new and different? She sighed out a deep breath.

There was only one way to find out.

She swallowed and turned to Lynée over the crackles from above. "Be right back," she said.

She took Guy's hand. "Follow me."

A brief pause accompanied his stare, but then he smiled. "Okay."

She led him through the maze of foldable chairs and blankets to the back of the park at the treeline. She stopped under a tree and pivoted to look up into his sparkling eyes.

"Everything okay?" he asked, his face more curious than concerned.

"Guy, I really like working with you." She reached for his other hand in hers.

"I like working with you too. Thanks for helping make that happen."

She gnawed the inside of her cheek. "I was wondering, would our working relationship be damaged if I kissed you?"

His sight traveled to her lips and back again. "I'm willing to risk it if you are."

Damn, hearing those words...it took all her focus not to jump into the deep end right then. She licked her lips and stepped closer. She rose to her tiptoes and placed a small kiss on his lips, then another. The hard cider and cinnamon lingered on his mouth. Her heart pounded in her chest. She lowered herself down and exhaled.

Guy's hands slid up her arms. He cupped her jaw and tipped up her head. Slowly, he lowered his lips over hers.

So firm, so inviting. She wanted more.

He grazed over her bottom lip with the tip of his tongue, and her lips parted. She loved how he dove in, searching her, reaching for her. She gripped his upper arms, sinking more into his kiss.

Their lips fused together as Guy tilted his head, taking things deeper. Tongues danced and moved as if they never had a perfect kiss until now. The firework booms dissipated into soft thuds that could've been her own heartbeat.

Yeah, this is something different, all right.

Guy's arms wrapped around her torso, melding their bodies together.

She moaned at the feeling of his arousal pressed against her. She gripped the back of his neck as the kiss turned passionate, desperate. The wetness gathered at the apex of the thighs, and she cursed the crowd around them.

He broke the kiss and panted. "Shit." He swallowed. "Had I known it would be like that, I'd have done that weeks ago."

She dropped her head and chuckled into his shoulder. "Absolutely." To hell with testing waters. Life was too short to be so cautious. She looked up and said the one thing that came to her mind. "Stay with me tonight."

He blew out a long breath. "Fuck, Skye, I would love nothing more. Nothing. But I can't tonight."

Her heart instantly woke up from its daydream. He didn't feel *that* way like she'd thought.

"When I said you shouldn't be alone—"

She laid her fingertips over his lips. "I know. And Lynée agreed to spend the night, but I just thought—" She lifted a shoulder, searching for the right words.

"I know. Believe me, I know." His thumb smoothed over her jawline, and he lowered his lips to hers for a shorter, less-passionate kiss.

He was being a gentleman. She'd forgotten what those guys looked like. Now that he'd reminded her, she wouldn't fault him for it.

"C'mon. Let's go watch the finale."

CHAPTER 10

REED SPRAWLED OUT on his mattress and stared up at the wood ceiling. Despite the phenomenal week in terms of his investigation, he had only one thing on his mind—Skye. He'd never known there could be such pleasure in just a kiss.

At the festival that night, she'd asked him to stay with her. Shit, how he wanted to. His dick was screaming for it.

But after the run-in with Vance, he couldn't take advantage of her. The bastard had shaken her to her core, and to her credit, she recovered nicely, but that wasn't Reed's make-up. Maybe after there was some distance from the asshole, so fresh on her mind.

More than likely, Vance had found her through her social media pics. So he wasn't exactly lying to Skye with that prediction. But in all honesty, there was another reason behind not wanting his own picture taken.

Facial recognition software was much more advanced than people realized. Adding sunglasses and letting his beard grow out for the Seattle trips wouldn't work well enough for some of the more sophisticated software. The last thing he wanted was for tech-savvy cartel thugs to find him through an innocent photo on Skye's social media. It would lead vicious psychos right to her front door. That

LocoLobo guy from the Dark Inferno game could easily find him that way if he'd learned Reed's name by now. Which is why Reed always had his camera covered with a piece of masking tape on every laptop and tablet he used. He made sure his burner phone didn't have a camera either. Just to be safe.

He grabbed the candle he bought and opened the lid. The crab apple smell was strong, reminding him so much of their awesome afternoon. More vividly, their kiss during the fireworks. He chuckled to himself. Fireworks during a kiss. A bit of a cliché, but that pounding of his heartbeat in time with the finale while he tasted Skye's amazing lips...*damn*. He wanted to take it further.

He adjusted himself under the blanket. His mind played out the scenario so vividly—Skye flush with wanting, maybe some moans would escape when he brought her to orgasm. He would take it slow at first, make sure she could handle his size. But he would make it exquisite for her. She would be in his bed all night if he had his way.

Fuck, yes.

He would have to wait. Luckily, he was a patient man. Anything she needed, he would do it.

Skye stepped out of the bathroom dressed in her comfy flannel pajamas and sat next to Lynée on her couch. Her cinnamon apple candle burned a beautiful glow in front of them, filling the air with her favorite scent.

"Care to share what happened with Guy tonight? You came back all flushed." Her best friend pushed her glasses up on her nose, cupping a mug of herbal tea.

Skye couldn't stop the blush she felt warm her cheeks. "I kissed him. Well, he kissed me. Okay, we kissed each other."

"I see." Lynée grinned. "How long were you planning that?"

Skye shook her head. "No planning. It just...happened. Something came over me. Like sitting there, all I wanted to do was be close to him."

"Are you falling in love with him?"

She smiled at the thought. "I think so. Frankly, the incident tonight with Vance might have just tipped me over the edge. I'm definitely infatuated."

"Really? I would've expected that to turn you off from men completely."

"That's what I thought too. But Guy had the opposite effect." She turned on the cushion to face her directly. "I'm sure I'm not going to explain this as well as you could. You always seem to know the right words. But...he was like gravity. Me circling him in this safe bubble. Or more like *I* was gravity, and he was circling *me*, giving me the distance I needed to still be me, but always within an arm's reach so I wasn't scared anymore. And he's not flashy or showy, but always makes me smile."

"Not to mention he became all Tarzan over you with Vance. I've never seen a man run off so fast, tripping over himself."

"Actually, Guy had a brilliant idea for the festival." Skye told her about the suggestion for a new booth, Whack-a-Dick.

They both laughed. Creative societal justice from the mind of creative chivalry.

"Guy was so awesome tonight, Lynnie."

"I know. Just swooped in and took control."

"Fearless. Like bullies are just fuel for his courage. As if nothing scares him. Wouldn't that be nice? Not to be afraid of anything."

Lynée set her hand on Skye's thigh. "You're pretty fearless in my eyes."

Skye scoffed. "I serve food in a diner day-in and day-out while reading books about courageous people. What's so fearless about that?"

"Hey." Lynée grabbed the decorative pillow behind her and swatted it against Skye's shoulder. "Enough self-deprecation. You just had an amazing day. Your ex ran for the hills, and you made out with your new crush. Not to mention, you get to hang out with me."

Skye stole the pillow and swatted her right back on the leg. "Fine." They laughed and finished their drinks.

"You should get some rest." Lynée set her mug on the coffee table and grabbed a book she brought over. Then cuddled down further on the sofa. "You have an early date with Mr. Fearless."

"Are you shunning me for a date with a book boyfriend? No doubt you'll read straight through to sunrise."

"No, just until two or three in the morning this time. Aside from church, I don't have anywhere else to be tomorrow."

Skye peered at the cover. "Is it something dirty?"

Lynée returned a knowing grin. "I'll let you read it when I'm finished. Give you some ideas for Guy."

She lowered her head to hide her blush. The thought of seeing Guy naked crossed her mind more than once. And she loved her imagination. "Lock up when you leave in the morning. Bookmark the steamy parts for me."

"That's *his* job." Lynée winked.

Nine a.m. couldn't come too soon. Reed wanted to

spend the entire day with Skye, looked forward to it like a kid on Christmas morning.

Joe would've called him a pussy, but he didn't care. Reed was having a monumental week on all fronts. The investigation was moving forward at full speed, he'd thwarted a bully, and Skye had set off fireworks in his heart. It was as if she'd woken him from a long nightmare. Pulling up to her house, with her blooming fall flowers, a wreath on the door, and a frog statue on the porch steps, he knew it was gonna be a good day.

"Hello, stranger." She greeted him on the porch with one of her glowing smiles. She wore a bright purple long-sleeve T-shirt and snug jeans that made casual look sexy. The ones that clung tight to her voluptuous ass. His favorite. She'd worn them several times when she'd change after the diner closed and she wasn't going straight home. It was all Reed could do to keep from staring.

"Morning, sunshine. Ready to go?"

"Yup. Let me grab my bag."

As he waited, he sauntered up the steps to inspect the flowers she'd just watered. Something vanilla filled the cooler air, coming from the ones that looked like daisies, only bigger. He'd never considered growing flowers or plants himself, not much point with his career field. But ones beautiful like this might change his mind.

Skye returned with a canvas tote around her shoulder. Her skin was so delectable, so soft, and her eyes filled with extra shine.

"You have a green thumb."

She glanced at the flowerpots and shrugged. "Another great use for books. Teaches me how to make pretty things."

He held out his arm for her to take it. "Mission accomplished."

Once in his truck, he turned on the engine. "Where are we headed?"

"Go toward downtown, and I'll tell you where to turn."

"Sounds good."

After the short drive, they pulled into a dirt parking lot at one of the orchards open to the public for the festival. The lot was already half full.

They walked through the gate, and Skye leaned down to retrieve a basket. "We pay by the bushel. Let's see if we can venture deeper, get away from the crowds."

She grabbed his hand, and Reed walked beside her, taking in his surroundings—rows and rows of green trees, people plucking apples from low-hanging branches, and kids directing dads to "that one there." A few people used the scattered ladders to pick the treasures on the higher boughs. Every step heightened the apple scent and woodsy aroma.

"Is this your first time?" she asked.

"Yeah. What a cool thing to do on a Sunday."

"Let's start here." Skye stopped in front of a tree full of ripe red apples.

He stood at the base, the branches reaching farther up than first glance. "Not sure it's tall enough." He smirked.

She chuckled.

The longer they picked, the hungrier he grew. He couldn't resist. He wiped an apple with the tail of his T-shirt and took a bite of the crisp fruit. "So juicy."

"Hey. You can't do that," Skye scolded.

"Really? But what if it's really good?" He closed the gap between them and brought the apple to within an inch of her lips. "Try it."

"We could get in trouble. We're supposed to pay for them first." The glimmer in her eyes betrayed the fun he knew she was having.

He brought the apple back a few inches. "Every good thief needs an accomplice. If it's not you, then who?" He kept his face as serious as he could muster while looking down at her gorgeously curved lips.

She stepped flush to his body and rested her hands on his waist. "You're convincing. Lay it on me."

He brought the apple close. Her lips parted. Damn if he wouldn't rather kiss them.

She closed her lips over the ripe apple and sank her teeth in. Her eyes fluttered closed. "Mmm. Delicious."

He watched until her eyes opened, then he lowered to place a simple kiss over her lips.

The apple's juices lingered on her mouth, sweet and tangy. He licked her top lip. So savory.

More to come. He gave her a smile. "Told you."

"Indeed. Now, back to work. We have more fun planned today."

And hopefully tonight.

They each carried a bushel back to the front of the orchard, happy with their loot. He paid for both baskets.

"What the heck am I supposed to do with all these apples?" he joked.

"What do you think? Keep what you can eat, and I'll take the rest to Rock Road and make stuff. This may shock you, but Ralph makes a great apple cider beef stew. I'm gonna fix some southern fried apples from my mom's recipe. Do you know how to make apple crisp or applesauce? Or how about caramel apple pork chops or apple stuffed chicken breast, or how about pumpkin-apple muffins?"

He slammed the tailgate of his pickup truck and grinned. "Okay, I think I got it, Bubba Gump."

She chuckled. "Off to town. The parade is about to start."

A parade. Baking apple goods. He could only smile. He felt like such a civilian, like a regular guy doing regular things. He would enjoy it while it lasted.

Which is when it hit him. He hadn't scanned for followers since they arrived at the orchard. He was getting comfortable; *she* made him comfortable.

As much as he loved the feeling, he had to be more alert.

Leading him by the hand, Skye found them a great spot along Main Street in just enough time for the parade. The festivities kicked off with the high school drumline—the percussion sound bouncing off the buildings. Several homemade floats wheeled past, most giving homage to the state fruit. Bicycles, tricycles, and scooters scuttled down the street by fearless children, the handles, and wheels decorated in more fall regalia. The high school band marched down the street with their flag corp and stopped half-way for several songs. Followed by the football team and cheerleaders. The local veterans' group and the auxiliary league had their own flatbeds pulling a group of members. Miss Washington followed, sitting in the back of a black convertible Mustang. Lastly, the mayor and his wife pulled up the rear in a 1960 Lincoln Continental convertible, red with a white leather interior.

"Freakin' awesome." Even Reed could appreciate the beautiful antique car's impressive condition.

"Nice, huh? He brings that out every year."

He looked at her sparkling eyes. "Are all small-town events like this?"

"Ours is."

All the faces he scanned were full of smiles, none of

them casting suspicious glares or searching for him. No weapons in anyone's hands, just cotton candy sticks, and balloon strings.

Wow, he really could get used to this life.

"Now, let's meander to the booths and see if we can find anything interesting for lunch." Skye smoothed her blonde hair behind her ear. "If you'd like, I have lasagna for dinner."

Reed's mouth instantly watered. "Do you grow your own basil and herbs for the sauce? After a day like today, I'd expect nothing less."

She smirked at his obvious jest. "And I churned my own butter after milking the cow in my backyard. Since you place additional demands on me, would you like to heat up your own microwave meal at your place instead?"

He laughed, curling her fingers between his. He kissed her knuckles. "I'm happy to milk the cow for you next time. And churn the butter. For more time in your company."

"That's much better." She chuckled, continuing down the street, their hands tangled together.

He could hardly believe the turn his life had taken in just a few short weeks. He had himself an invitation to dine with his favorite person, a home-cooked dinner with a beautiful, vivacious woman. Things were finally looking up in his world, after so long in darkness.

Skye unlocked her front door as Guy followed her in carrying her basket of apples.

"You can set them here." She pointed to a place out of the way in her kitchen. She would go through those later, make a few things she could freeze, then bring the rest to Rock Road.

She turned on the oven and pulled the lasagna out of

the fridge.

Her house was an older, quaint rental owned by a family friend. Emphasis on old. She really wanted to replace the Formica countertops, but considering it was temporary, she wouldn't bother. Renting kept her from being tied to this town any more than necessary.

Two dark beams stretched across the high-vaulted ceilings into the living room that reminded her of a log cabin resort, cozy and grand at the same time. The island was topped with butcher block wood, inspired by a DIY television show she often watched, so at least the space had a few modern things going for it. Not to mention the clear crystal cabinet knobs she installed herself.

Seeing Guy in her house, perusing her sanctuary, made her suddenly nervous. Anxious for what was to come but also wondering if he'd like her home. What expectations did he have? More importantly, what were her own?

Easy, Skye. Focus on one thing at a time.

"Nice place." He pulled her from her stray thoughts. "Suits you."

"Thanks. I wouldn't mind doing some updating, but I'm just renting."

She glanced at the oven, then back at Guy. "I really need to take a shower. Would you mind putting this in the oven when the thermostat dings and set the timer for an hour?"

"No problem. Would you like me to milk the cow out back while you're busy?" He grinned.

Skye chuckled. "She's sleeping right now. But there's plenty of butter to churn in the fridge. Along with some wine and beer." She winked. "Make yourself comfortable. I'll be right back."

She scampered back to her bedroom, leaning against

the door after it closed.

The man was actually in her house. Her heart thumped wildly, and her expectations of what would happen after the meal swirled in her mind in high-definition. She could finally have Guy all to herself. Just him and her, and she didn't have to share him with anyone or be interrupted by customers. She'd woken early, thinking of only him.

Sometimes she really didn't have the ability to go slow. Right now, she didn't want to be cautious and test the waters. Whatever came next with Guy, she wanted to high-dive into it. Yes, she'd been burned before, but life was too damn short. What if this feeling with him was real? What if he was exactly what she hoped for, the nice guy with honest intentions that lit her up inside? That wanted to dive into the deep end right beside her? What would her novels say about this level of obsession? She could barely breathe with the anticipation.

She stripped and entered the bathroom, then twisted the shower lever to hot. She doused her body, letting the warmth envelope her. She may be getting ahead of herself, but she wanted Guy. She'd dreamt about him, fantasized about him, and simply couldn't get him out of her mind.

Lynée may be onto something about her being in love. She wasn't sure about that. But whatever it was called, she wanted it. All of it. She wanted him; she could almost taste it.

She rinsed out her conditioner, shut off the water, and reached for a towel.

A knock came at the door.

"Just a minute." She wrapped a towel around herself.

The door opened.

She gasped.

Guy stood before her, his eyes examining her from

head to toe. "I'm sorry. I thought you said, 'I'm finished.'" He simply stared at her, like he'd never seen a wet woman in a towel before.

Heat flushed her cheeks.

Should I push him out? She just stood there, waiting for him to move. To say something. To leave. Although the idea of him leaving made her heart sink.

Finally, he moved closer. Grabbing a hand towel from the rod, he patted her cheeks and forehead dry. He grazed the towel over her lips.

Her body involuntarily leaned into it. He could probably see her heartbeat through her skin, it was pounding so hard.

He tilted down and grazed his lips across hers. Sweet, timid, questioning.

Her stomach flipped over, and she stood there, soaking up his every caress.

The towel in his hand traveled down her neck and across her upper chest. His butterfly kisses followed the path, searing along her skin in the most delicious recipe for seduction.

She sighed, desperate for breath. Amazing how these light touches could suck all oxygen from the tiny bathroom and melt her into a puddle. But she didn't want him to stop, so she didn't dare move.

He moved up her neck and returned to her lips. This time he kissed her deeper, passionately.

She opened for him, their tongues melding with each other.

Oh yeah.

Tilting her head, she urged him deeper. Her hands rested on his chest as she leaned into him, moaning into his mouth.

Yes, this is what fearless is for.

He pulled back. His face was flushed, probably just as much as hers. His swollen lips were plump and ripe. "I've wanted to do that all day." His twinkling eyes turned a rich chocolate brown.

Damn. She wanted to do that all over again.

He brought the towel to her arm and stroked it up and down, oh so slowly. His hand moved over her clavicle to her other arm, repeating the movements. "Turn around," he whispered.

She presented him with her back. The fogged mirror streaked with droplets of accumulated condensation obscured their reflection. She had only touch to rely on, and she would relish everything he did.

He dried her left shoulder, swiping across her upper back, sweeping her hair over her right shoulder. With his free hand, he gave her towel a little tug.

She bit her lip and released one corner. The bath sheet slid off her back and loosely fell across the front of her body. Her whole backside was naked, revealed to his feasting eyes. Her sex started to ache.

He placed a kiss on her mid-back and sunk down to dry her legs.

Surely he wouldn't try and dry her *there,* would he?

His hands crept higher, the towel slowly moving up to her ass.

She whimpered.

Although the hand towel went up the inside of her leg to the apex of her thighs, he didn't linger. He placed a kiss on her ass cheek and rose.

Skye let out the breath she'd held. The flush of heat to her face made her dizzy.

He made another pass over her back and farther up.

Wrapping the towel around her dripping hair, he squeezed.

The pressure was exquisite.

Suddenly, he stopped. Warmth left her body as she realized he'd stepped back.

She looked over her right shoulder. "What is it?"

His fingertips ran over the back of her shoulder, lingering on one spot. "Is this...from the stairs? From Vance?"

Her breath hitched. She'd forgotten about her scar. Over time, her gaze had been trained to ignore it.

The air around them turned tense.

"It doesn't hurt."

He didn't say a thing. The tension, however, billowed off him like the wind from the summit of Mount Washington.

She gripped her towel and pivoted to face him. "I'm fine, Guy."

He shook his head. "He's an asshole."

"He is, and life goes on. But you're thinking too hard. C'mon. Lasagna solves everything." She pushed on her tiptoes and pecked his lips, praying this wouldn't ruin their night. After the appetizer he'd just given her, she really didn't want him to leave.

She walked into her bedroom and reached in her closet for a T-shirt and pink and taupe camo pants. Guy closed the doors to the bathroom for privacy.

After a few quick minutes of lotion and makeup, and twirling her hair into a damp braid, she met him in the kitchen, sipping on a glass of red wine.

"May I have a glass," she asked with a glance at the timer.

From the creases in his forehead, Guy was still thinking about Vance as he poured a second glass of wine.

Time to redirect.

"So, I'd like to think of this as a date. Maybe a first date."

The creases smoothed. The corners of his lips quirked up as did an eyebrow.

"On dates, people get to know each other. I know what you told me about coming to Cascade Creek, but I want the *real* answer. I'd told you a lot about my past, I think it's only fair."

His chest rose and fell, filling his lungs with air. "That might dampen the mood." He set the glass on the island but didn't pull back his hand.

"Well..." She took the glass and raised it to her lips. "Unless you're a serial killer intending on making me your next victim, then I think you should still take the chance."

After a few moments of silence and twirling his wine glass between his fingers, he spoke. "I came up here to process and escape. For some quiet. A while ago, I lost my best friend. My mentor. I picked this area because I used to go fishing here with my uncle as a little kid. After everything I saw...this was the first place that came to mind for peace and quiet."

"I'm so sorry. What happened?'

His grip tightened around the wine glass, and it was a long moment before he answered. "He was shot in the line of duty. It's still hard to talk about."

Skye nodded. *In the line of duty.* So he was law enforcement of some kind. Or used to be. Pressing him with questions wasn't a good idea. Of all people, she knew time was the best healer. Processing was a time game. Eventually, talking about it made it all better. But only when one was ready.

"What about your parents? Brothers and sisters?"

He shook his head. "No siblings. Dad has dementia, and I don't want to burden my mom with this. When I'm ready, I'll reach out."

She couldn't even imagine what Guy must have gone through. If she lost Lynée—God, she didn't even want to think about it.

CHAPTER 11

WHAT A WAY to kill an erection. One minute Reed had accidentally walked in on dripping-wet Skye wrapped in a towel he was gently ridding her of. The next minute he could see nothing but blazing red as anger boiled inside him over that asshole Vance. That scar on Skye's shoulder only made him wish he'd at least bloodied Vance's nose the previous day.

Then she'd nudged him on his past. Which only reminded him of the real reason he was up here in the first place. Another buzzkill.

Protecting Skye wasn't just about his job or justice. And he knew it. Skye stirred something more in him, something of which he didn't want to let go.

But she had a point—life goes on.

She was living proof that someone can move on after life drops a bucket of shit over their heads.

The thought had never occurred to him before. To move on. Move on to what?

What was he supposed to do "after"? After he caught the bad guy?

Skye waved a hand over his blank stare. "You're doing it again. Thinking way too hard."

He forced a playful smile. "Sorry."

"We have a few minutes. Want to help me set the table?" She gathered silverware and plates and handed them to him. "Where did you learn to cook?"

Reed stopped and turned his head to lock eyes with her. "University of YouTube and Google. Skye, I'm not much of a cook, if you couldn't tell." He continued setting out the plateware.

Her eyes rounded. "Really?" She shifted her weight on one hip and studied him. "You took that job because you were desperate."

He shrugged.

"Damn. You learned all those dishes on the fly? You're a quick study."

He twirled a fork around his fingers before setting it down. "Thanks. I'm a big gamer, so I look at it like a game." He grabbed his wine glass and sipped. "Strategy, timing, placement, multi-tasking—all the same principles apply."

"You should teach Ralph how to cook. Otherwise, you're not allowed to leave. Ever." She grinned. "Is there anything you're not good at?"

That was a loaded question. He resisted saying *Not a damn thing when it comes to you.*

Her hand flew up to stop him, as if she could hear the words in his head, and she chuckled. "Never mind. Forget I asked."

Before he could capitalize on the moment, the oven timer went off. At least he had a pile of food before him to distract his libido. On the first mouthful, his taste buds came alive. The bite was thick with cheese and meat, and not too hot. "Delicious."

She smiled. "Thanks."

"Ralph should employ you to be the chef."

"Then what job would you have? The waiter? You're

pretty good with the customers, all that charm and suave. But could you handle the bristly ones with extra demands and little patience?"

"Sure." He scooped the last forkful from his plate. "If you were behind the counter, all I have to do to lift my spirits is look at you."

She grabbed her wine. "Smooth."

The earlier rage from seeing her scar had dissipated, and just sitting back with his wine glass and looking over at his delectable date made him content. More than content. "Where did you learn to make scrumptious things like this?"

She wiped her mouth with a napkin. "My mom. She loves to cook."

"Any brothers and sisters?" He shoveled in another bite.

"Nope, only child. Lynée too, which I think explains why we're so close. Both starved for sisterhood."

Skye's phone lit up with a text from Lynée.

Speak of a church lady.

She read from her phone. "The new Baldacci novel came in, and Lynée offered to hold it for me."

His ears perked up at that one. Her fingers flew over the screen to text a reply, but he couldn't help himself. Being able to read a new mystery novel before this book-addict across from him knew the ending was more than tempting.

Reed struck like a snake pulling the phone from her fingers.

"Hey! Give that back." Her sporting grin made him chuckle.

Damn, he loved to play with her, and he equally loved this author. "Uh-uh. Not until you let me read it first."

She lunged forward to grab the phone, but he held it behind him out of reach.

Her eyes narrowed, barely concealing that beautiful sparkle. "You dare to hold my phone hostage, after all this yumminess I fed you, so you can get a book that's rightfully mine?"

He licked his lips, barely able to hold back the temptation. "What are you going to do about it?"

She jumped out of her chair and grabbed his elbow to pull down his arm.

He was quicker and stronger. Skye tried so hard to pull down his arm, both of them laughing. She got a little too close, so he stood up and backed away.

"I get the book first. My friend, my book." She followed.

"Nope, it's my phone now. I think I'll tell her you're so graciously giving it to me first."

"No way." She lunged again, and he stepped back, bumping into the sofa.

She's good.

"You almost had it that time, precious. Don't give up."

The flush in her cheeks made her damn-near irresistible.

She heaved herself toward him once again. This time, using the momentum of her body, he wrapped an arm around her torso, spun them both, and had her on her back against the sofa cushions. His hips pinned her below him.

His sight traveled to her lips then to her eyes. He waited for a protest, but she merely stared back, panting in surprise.

Why was he distracting himself with this little game? He had to finish his research. Find Joe's killer and be on his way. But damn, he was so hungry for this. For her.

Her phone dropped to the floor.

He claimed her lips in a way he'd been craving all

damn day.

Her soft lips relented easily, kissing him back with equal vigor.

His lips possessed her, sprinkling kisses down her warm neck. His erection grew with every pant and moan. He had to have her.

Her labored breath floated past his ear as her fingers tunneled through his hair.

"Guy," she whispered.

He nearly flinched at the name. Her fiery gaze told him not to stop. With a grasp on the hem of her T-shirt, he yanked it over her head and flung it behind them. His shirt followed.

The nude satin bra displayed her delectable cleavage, her breasts so supple and inviting.

"Skye, I want you so badly," he whispered, lust coating his voice. "Tell me now if you want to stop. Because if you say it later, I might not hear you."

"Don't stop. Please." Her hands stroked over his chest to his jaw, her skin so soft and delicate. "I want you. I want to feel you."

Thank God in heaven.

He took her mouth in a desperate, passionate kiss, dancing with her tongue like he was starving for her. With a deft hand, he reached behind her back and unsnapped her bra, dropping it with the other items.

He leaned down, admiring her nipples puckering with desire. So pink and plump, straining for him. He suckled her beautiful breasts. The arch in her back as she reached for more urged him on.

Reed taunted her further trailing his hand down her soft belly to her pants. Loosening the button and zipper, the enticing feminine scent washed over him. Even better than the soap she'd bought at the festival.

With a firm grip on her underwear and pants, he jerked the garments off like a man on a singular, sultry mission.

Her beautiful body was too gorgeous to resist. The polyester uniform he was used to seeing her in hid most of her smooth curvy figure, and tonight his eyes could feast on her full shape. Tonight, she was all his. For once, he thanked his lucky-ass stars.

He slid a finger through her wet slit. Oh, so slick and silky.

She mewled.

"Fuck, Skye. You're so wet." He didn't waste another second. With a quick lift, he pushed her farther up the sofa. Then with his hands on her thighs, he crouched between her legs and licked straight up her core to her swollen clit.

She cried out, grabbing hold of his head as he made love to her sex.

He circled and lapped at her nub while he slowly pushed in a finger, eliciting more moaning. She tasted so sweet. His dick was screaming to plunge inside, but taking his time was important. She needed this. He slid in another finger and pumped steadily. Her sexy sounds escalating higher with every moment made him greedy for more, to have her clench around him. Her legs squeezed his head with the building tension, her hips rolling to the rhythm of his tongue. That pressure never felt so welcome. After a few short moments, her muscles contracted around him.

"Oh. Oh, God," she called out. Warmth surged into his mouth, her sweet and tangy succulence.

Hell yes.

He held tight to her waist as she writhed below him, wringing every last ounce of pleasure she could stand.

Reed couldn't wait anymore. He whipped open his fly

and pushed them down, freeing his rigid dick. Fishing out the rubber from his back pocket, he sheathed himself, his hands shaking from his fervor. Leaning over Skye, he aligned himself at her entrance. He held her hands over her head and wove his fingers through hers.

She wrapped her legs around his waist. Damn, she looked so beautiful, her face so flush from her first climax, and her neck glistening.

With his lips scant inches above hers, he whispered, "Are you ready?"

She nodded and panted, "Yes."

Thank God. "I want you like I've never wanted anything else in my life."

As he claimed her lips, he claimed her body. Pushing hard and fast, he swallowed her gasp. He pulled back his hips and plunged in again, taking all he could. His body propelled faster and harder on its own, with barely any control. That was how crazy she drove him. Like a puppeteer to a marionette.

From her gasps and the open circle of her mouth, he prayed he wasn't hurting her.

"Oh God, Guy, more. Please more. You feel...so incredible."

"So do you, baby. We're taking all night." He continued, his balls tightening with each thrust. "This is just the beginning." He couldn't hold on any longer. With a groan, he released deep inside her, fireworks detonating throughout his entire body.

He collapsed, panting into her shoulder. Only when he didn't feel dizzy anymore, he edged her to the side and pulled her body flush to his. He'd need a little time to recuperate before he started another round. Damn, she'd turned him into an addict.

"Holy shit, Guy." Skye wiggled her breasts against his chest, her body so warm and responsive. "That was so worth the risk."

Shit. Guilt from not being forthright about his name sobered his lustful mini-coma. Damn, he so desperately wanted to tell her his real name. To hear "Reed" on her lips... But then he'd have to spill the whole truth. Which would send her running.

He forced himself to quash those feelings and just buried his face in her neck. Hoping it wasn't written all over his face. He'd been upfront about everything else with Skye, except for this. He hated lying to her, but it couldn't be helped. He wouldn't let this ruin their night.

Someday, when all this was resolved, he would tell her. If it would ever be resolved. Hopefully.

The salacious delight spread over Skye like a warm blanket. She lay on her sofa, eyes closed, and Guy's breath drifting across her hair. Oh, how she loved his muscular chest pressed against hers. And the buzz of the best sex she'd ever had still hummed through her body.

"Wow," she breathed. Guy had barely been out of her a minute, and she couldn't wait for more.

"Yeah." He pressed his lips to her forehead, letting them linger. "As much as I don't want to disrupt this, maybe *I* should jump in the shower."

She chuckled. "Okay. That'll give me time to clean up."

He hoisted his body up and paused, hovering over her, meeting her gaze. "Damn, you're beautiful."

"Just keep saying that. It works for me." She chuckled and held out her hand. He helped her stand and pulled her in for another hug.

"Five minutes. Meet me right back here, okay?"

Her insides fluttered. "It's a date."

His lips curled up at the corners, and he made his way down the hall.

"Towels are in the closet," she called after him.

She sighed as she dressed and cleared the table.

God. When had sex ever been so good?

Maybe it never was. Maybe this was it, the Holy Grail.

Can a person have a sexual soul mate?

She scoffed and carried the plates to the sink. *Ridiculous. The pheromones were screwing with her brain cells.*

Okay, she was arguing with herself, which was equally ridiculous. But it was as if the room suddenly brightened. Bigger and the world simultaneously more hopeful.

As she washed the dishes at the sink, her skin woke up with his presence. His energy pulsed through the air behind her. He awakened parts of her she missed having worshiped by a man. And *this* man knew just how to worship her.

"Who said you could get dressed?" he whispered at her back.

She grinned. "I didn't know I needed permission. I mean, how crazy is it to wash dishes naked?"

"Lovely Skye, you can't focus on a simple task like this while you're naked?" He started caressing the skin under her shirt, laying kisses against her neck. "I've seen your multi-tasking skills at the diner." He reached around her and unbuttoned her pants. Pulled down the zipper. "You're masterful. Juggling tables and orders. Coffee refills with conversation." He lifted her arms and pulled her shirt over her head.

A familiar slickness grew at the apex of her thighs. Her breath shallowed.

Before her hands returned to the soapy water, he

unlatched her bra and dropped it. Her pants and underwear were next. In a heartbeat, she was naked at her kitchen sink.

Guy's towel didn't hide his erection pressed against her backside. His hands slid over her hips, up her torso, cupping her breasts and playing with her peeked nipples.

A moan echoed across the kitchen, and she let her head lull back onto his shoulder.

"Don't let me distract you. Dip your hands in the soap while I pleasure you. Unless that would bother you."

She wanted to laugh out loud. *Bother* wasn't exactly the word she would use.

His deft fingers toyed with her nipples as he sucked and licked the side of her neck, making it damn-near impossible to concentrate.

A simple twist and tug of her nipples sent a rush of hot nectar to her nether lips. "Oh God," she breathed.

His hands grazed down the side of her body and over her ass cheeks.

She desperately wanted to squeeze her legs together to stave off the ache building inside with a glorious fury.

With his knees, he pushed her legs further apart.

Her own knees shook slightly, and she grabbed the counter to steady herself.

Guy caressed her thighs inside and out but never touched where she ached the most.

"Don't you think that pot is clean now?" he whispered at her ear.

Right. She rinsed the pot, not caring if it was clean or dirty. She was desperate to have Guy inside her.

Finally, the tips of two fingers slid easily through her wet slit, spreading the moisture over her lips.

"Oh my."

He pulled her back from the sink one step. "This

shouldn't be much of an imposition. Is it, Skye?" She could hear the smile in his voice.

He was playing with her, building her up, teasing her, not giving her what she desired.

She whimpered.

His fingertips slid over her sex again, and this time he slid them higher. Right through—oh, God—her ass cheeks.

Oh heavens! She grabbed the side of the counter, a gasp lodged in her throat. But it felt *so good*. Being so dirty in the process of cleaning. That pressure...that building heat... She shouldn't like that so much.

She wanted to arch more, push back against him, but she dared not move.

Concentrate. She washed her spatula and rinsed it under the faucet.

The soft cotton of his towel brushed against her ankles, where it pooled at her feet.

He was naked too. Then the condom wrapper ripped open.

Yes!

His magnificent erection glossed over her wet core, one pass, then another.

"Are you ready for another round?"

"Mm, yes." Her voice was so breathy.

Finally, with his hands spreading her apart, he pushed inside.

They both moaned.

Her eyelids dropped closed as she savored the exquisite feeling of Guy's cock pushing against her vaginal walls.

He pumped a few times, then pulled out.

Her eyes flew open. "What—"

"Sweet Skye. I'm concerned I'm distracting you.

Perhaps I should stop."

Bastard. "No. I'm good." She reached for a lid. Only a few pieces left.

With a small chuckle, he began kissing her again, starting at her neck, trailing down her back with small nips. He went to his knees behind her, and with another pull at her hips, she stepped back more—giving him access to her achy sex.

"Does this make you want to come?" His tongue smoothed over her clit, swirling this way and that with a flat tongue.

She moaned, "Hell yes." Her heart pumped double-time.

Wash. Rinse.

His tongue swirled and flicked, making her raw with need.

He stood, pulling her hair away from her shoulder.

"You are so beautiful. I want to hear you come." His shaking hands clasped her hips. With a groan, he drove into her.

Oh, thank God. Her channel tightened around him, and it was as if her whole body sighed. She could tell stringing it out for her was about to kill him. Served him right. This slow, teasing, almost torturous lovemaking needed to be reciprocal.

Pumping slow and controlled, the orgasm she'd craved threatened to claw its way to the surface. So close... Just a few more, and she'd shatter.

He pulled out again and dropped to his knees, his mouth worshipping her sex.

"Ah." She'd forgotten to keep cleaning. All the magical things he was doing to her body wiped her memory.

Wash. Rinse.

Guy pushed two fingers inside her, circled his thumb over her burgeoning clit, and sucked a spot at the base of her ass.

Her knees nearly buckled. He made life dizzying, delicious, and oh so unexpected.

Amazing.

"How does that feel, Skye? Do you want more?"

"More," she panted. The ceiling started to spin.

He added more pressure, sucking harder with that incredible tongue.

That tipped her over the edge. She cried out. And splintered apart, gripping the edge of the counter. Waves of shimmering joy shot throughout her body.

He stood and, with his hands holding her tightly, he dove deep inside her. Ramming the end of her nearly split her apart. He thrust several more times, and that pulsing coil inside her tightened again, much faster than she imagined. Before long, another orgasm detonated from her core.

"Unh." The glorious release unraveled her from the inside out. She slumped against the sink, completely unable to hold up her own weight.

Guy growled and wrapped his right arm around her waist, his left hand braced on the counter. His breath labored against her back.

Her panting slowed. "I'd think I'd died and gone to heaven, except I'm pretty sure there's no dish-detail behind the pearly gates."

He chuckled and kissed between her shoulder blades. "Perfect."

It certainly was.

At this point, Skye was more than damn sure. Guy wasn't just a fleeting infatuation, nor was she enamored with an enigma passing through. This man not only owned her body. He owned her heart.

CHAPTER 12

RENEWED WITH EXTRA vigor from the amazing Sunday with Skye, Reed forced himself to focus on work the following day. The diner was closed the Monday after the festival, so he didn't have to go in. He would've rather spent the whole day making love to Skye in her bed. He found himself insatiable with her. But he had to concentrate on his case. To move the needle on identifying Joe's murderer.

Luckily, she was like a fountain of youth on his motivation. His fingers flew across the keyboard faster, and he thought more clearly. When he hit a dead-end, it didn't frustrate him. He just maneuvered around it.

By the end of his twenty-four-hour-straight research session on the computer, coffee grounds and microwave meals filled his trash can.

Reed pushed forward on Joe's game, Dark Inferno, and managed to uncover the IP address and physical location of every player on the chat sessions. Even several with images of the players themselves through their computer cameras, completely unaware they were monitored. Most were dead ends. Legitimate players of the game with no connection to his case.

The few smart ones had their cameras blocked. Particularly LocoLobo, the one who'd threatened him. His was the first one Reed looked up. Several IP addresses were linked back to the same online retailer, from a single purchase order from one company. After a little more digging, it was a dummy corporation in Mexico. The game developer was through another dummy corporation also out of Mexico. Neither of them rang any bells from Reed's previous bank searches last year when he was knee-deep in the financials of the cartel's holdings. The game designer was listed as D. Huerta in California. But there were far too many D. Huerta's to look into.

Much of the information he needed was now only available in government databases. And *that* he would never dare search from his own home. He didn't have the equipment or processing capacity to defeat their security systems from this rental house without being caught. That would certainly bring other agents to his door in less than twenty minutes. Which was nowhere near enough time to conduct his search.

He'd have to make another trek out to Seattle. To conduct the fastest search he'd ever done. Because he had to be ready to run.

His fingers stopped on the keyboard. His heart sank. Once he was on the run, he couldn't come back here. He'd never see Skye again.

The thought made his heart crack.

The DEA would inevitably follow him. Leading them back to his hideout in the beautiful Cascade Mountains was unthinkable. Because then they would start digging for information on him, including interviewing everyone in town. Which meant Skye would learn the truth about him.

Damn, the woman had already been burned enough in her life, he didn't want to be the cause of more anguish. No, he couldn't do that. He ground his teeth.

Shit, there has to be another way.

He stood and paced the kitchen. His brain had started to turn to mush, and his leg muscles were like jelly. "Think, Reed. Think. There has to be another way."

How could he break into DEA's systems without compromising his location? The methods were out there, just far out of his capabilities with a ramen-noodle budget and second-hand equipment. Showing up at a DEA field office was out of the question, too. He'd be arrested on sight.

He needed another DEA agent's login. That way, he could search without having to rush. Obviously, he couldn't use Joe's, and his own was shut down long ago.

Looking up the agents out of the Seattle division to break into their personal computers would be easy enough for him, but would considerably lengthen the time to find this target. Or he could flood their servers with traffic, all at once. Give them thousands of other leads to trace, which would delay their response time. That might give him the cycles he needed on their systems. But that required preparation. And more computers.

He had to find a way. There was no other way to clear his name. It wasn't just enough to prove he didn't do it; he had to find the one who'd killed Joe. Turn that bastard over to the DEA on a platter, along with the evidence to prove he wasn't rogue. It was impossible to achieve any of that from a prison cell.

He started doing pushups on the kitchen floor, expending energy to get his brain rewired. After fifty, he moved to chin-ups on the overhead wooden beam. Which took standing on a chair and jumping up to grab the lowest one. After a set of those followed by some pull-ups, he was still far too antsy. He shut down all his systems except the security cameras, laced on his shoes, and threw on his ballcap.

A run was the second-best way to get this energy out and flood his brain with fresh oxygen. The best way to boost his energy required calling Skye for another amazing date, but he needed to save that for when he had a longer chunk of time. In fact, he'd use a call with Skye as his reward. Find the killer's location, then schedule another date with his infatuation.

But first, a quick run.

With a stretch of his legs, he trotted off down the long, gravel driveway.

The pine trees gave off a fresh scent that combined with the cool mountain air in an invigorating way. The rushing creek in the distance combined with the sound of his pounding feet created a rhythmic soundtrack. He never listened to music as he ran as much as he wanted to. He had to be on alert for someone coming up behind him. Constantly scanning his surroundings for anyone suspicious was innate. Despite how comfortable he felt here in Cascade Creek, he couldn't let his instincts become dulled. He turned onto the road, hugging the shoulder toward town.

Late afternoon sunlight filtered between the trees as he trekked down the mountain road. He almost couldn't handle the normalcy of the moment. Being able to just walk out one's door for a run without having to worry about being chased or caught on cameras... just enjoying the nature around him. He'd almost forgotten that feeling.

As strange as it was to him, he liked it. He wanted to get used to it. He wanted normalcy. Like a deployed soldier fighting hard to get home, only to realize the atrocities he'd seen made it difficult to fully adapt to the change.

Dammit, he didn't want to be like that. He didn't want

to admit that he probably suffered from some form of PTSD. Seeing his partner get shot would do that to anyone, let alone having to constantly be on the run, full-paranoia twenty-four seven for a full year. But sitting around, focusing on it wasn't the best way to handle it either.

He had to keep moving. He had to stay focused on the end goal. He'd worry about *after* if he ever got to see it.

The road curved around a bend then opened to a waterfall over a small cliff. Not too high, only about fifteen feet, but the rushing water sound enveloped his mind like a blanket. The water fell into the creek that meandered parallel to the road. Down the hill beyond a few apple and olive orchards, the courthouse bell tower stood tall among the other buildings nestled against the main road. Even from up here, Reed could see the children playing on the school playground. Teachers guided little kids into lines to go back into the building, where they'd finish their lessons, then go home to their families. Likely have dinner together around a table, and then parents help their children with homework. The usual bath, book, bed routine that 'normal' people experienced.

An image of Skye sitting across a table from him as they fed their children flitted into his mind. Her smile was bright, the same as on their daughter's, twirling her fork around a plate of spaghetti. He could even see the smudge of sauce on his son's face, which he'd wipe off with a napkin. His heart ached for that potential future. He dared to let himself smile.

The image transferred to the door busted into splinters. Skye's scream was piercing; her form huddled over their kids. The doorframe filled with the vicious face of that cartel assassin from the warehouse. The dark eyes, the demonic sneer...

He raised a black pistol, aimed directly at Skye, ...and fired.

Reed blinked. His heart raced on the top of that hill, the waterfall still crashing into the creek in front of him. The gunshot still rang in his ears. Almost as loud as the scream.

He pulled off his hat and wiped the cold sweat from his brow. He put that cap back on, backward this time. He continued jogging, focusing hard on the sound of his feet on the pavement.

He had no idea what the future held for him. But it sure as shit wouldn't be that one with Skye in the crosshairs. He wouldn't allow it.

Skye walked out of the classroom when her phone buzzed in her purse. *Guy*. She instantly smiled.

"Hi, stranger."

"Hi, beautiful. Hungry?"

"I am." She'd grabbed a protein drink from her fridge before heading out, but days like this, she'd have to eat a late dinner. She was pretty used to pulling something out of the freezer. Anything quick and easy.

"Good. I'm bringing dinner. I'll be there in thirty." The line went dead.

She smiled again. Short and to the point.

That's my man.

Her stomach did a backflip at the thought.

There was just enough time to drop her backpack on the bench, check her hair, and down a glass of water when the doorbell rang.

Guy stood at her door, holding a brown bag that smelled like barbeque. He looked just as yummy in his tight, black V-neck sweater and freshly shaved face.

"Don't you look delicious." She wiggled her eyebrows.

He strolled in slowly, eyeing her up and down. "So do you."

"Thank you." She opened the door wider and let him enter. "But you didn't sleep well last night."

"How can you tell?" He set the bag on her kitchen table.

"The creases in your forehead. You're wearing them a little too deep." She stepped closer and tried to wipe them from his skin.

"You're wearing my favorite jeans."

She grinned as she glanced down. "Your favorite?" She lifted her head to meet his gaze, and his eyes were the color of rich chocolate ganache. *Yummy!*

He moved closer, wrapping his hands over his hips as his thumbs stroked the space over her waistband. He kissed her briefly, his mouth lingering over hers.

Her breath came quicker. "It's good to see you, too."

"Dinner can wait."

She licked her lips, her mouth suddenly dry.

He brought her flush to his body, his arousal pressing on her low belly.

She tilted her head as he leaned down, his lips brushed against hers.

"Do you know why I love them so much?" His hand crept over her left ass cheek and squeezed. "Because they make your ass look so fucking delectable."

Moisture gathered at the apex of her thighs. Her hunger for food became a distant memory. She was hungry for Guy.

"Says the cook," she murmured.

"You know it." His hand slid down her thigh, lifting at the knee. He aligned their bodies in just the right way.

"Oh my," she breathed. Her hands flew to his shoulders for balance.

He easily lifted her mere inches off the floor and swung her toward the door. His body pressed her against the wood panels as his kisses trailed over her jaw and down her neck.

She stole a glance at her large front window. It was dusk, but still, anyone could look in and see them. "Guy, the window."

He raised his head to cast a glance at the uncovered window. "I don't care if they see us." He flipped off the light switch, and before she could protest, he grabbed the hem of her sweater and whipped it off her.

Oh, God. People would be able to see inside. Since when was Guy an exhibitionist? Skye wished she cared more, but right then, with his hungry mouth on her neck and collarbone, he was all she cared about.

"You must have really missed me this weekend," she panted.

"You're damn right I did." He kissed and licked his way south, pulling the bra straps off her shoulders.

She clutched his head, arching into his face and his warm, talented mouth.

He growled. He moved lower to her belly while unfastening her jeans.

Her breaths came quicker, and her face warmed. "What have you been doing all cooped up at your place?" She pushed against her waistband, helping him with his task. The need for him thrummed throughout her whole body, down to her fingertips.

She stepped out of the garments as Guy rose.

"Nothing as important as this."

She reached for his belt and began working on his clothes. When his zipper was open, she reached in and cupped him, wrapping her fingers around his length.

He growled again, letting his head fall back a few inches. The ecstasy on his face was palpable. She *loved* that look. "Fuck, Skye. I crave your touch. I crave you."

She gave him one last glance, pushed against his hips, signaling her next move. She slid down the door, and he stepped back, giving her all the room she needed.

His cock was so rigid, the head an eager reddish-purple with a tiny drop on the tip. With a firm grip at the base, she instantly took him in her mouth.

"Fuck," he breathed. He braced his hands against the door, leaning into her, letting her pleasure him.

She took him all the way in, as far as her throat would allow, and wrapped her tongue around him. Then slowly dragged out, sucking as she went. His skin was salty, and his semen tart. But what she loved most were his groans, the moans that proved she'd hit the right spot. She loved knowing she could make him feel this good.

After several more sucklings and cradling his balls, she felt his hands on her shoulders as he pulled out. "I need to be inside you." He took her hand, bringing her to standing. His lips crushed over hers as his hand tunneled between them, seeking her tender flesh. Testing her, teasing her.

As his finger grazed over her clit, she gasped. Her eyelids fell closed as he spread her slickness, building the anticipation for her. She widened her stance, and he drove two fingers inside her.

"Guy. Please," she begged, her muscles clenching around his digits.

He reached for a condom, ripping the package with his teeth, and sheathed himself. In one fluid movement, he cupped her ass cheeks, lifting her, aligned his cock to her entrance, and pushed in.

"Unh." Her head thunked against the door.

His thrusts rocked her up and down. The thumping against the wood door was no doubt easily heard outside. If anyone was passing by, they might be concerned. She didn't care.

She rode the waves higher and higher, closer to ecstasy. In this position, with her legs wrapped around him and her hips tilted forward, she reveled in taking all of him. She reveled in how intense it felt. Her breath came in quick pants as he dove in and pulled back, over and over, pushing her closer to climax.

"Skye, I can't get enough of you. I don't know if I'll ever get enough of you." His lips closed over her neck, sucking and licking.

"I'm all yours. Ah!" The beginning of an orgasm rose to the surface. "Don't stop, baby. Please."

His thrusts came faster, and grinding against him was the most natural thing in the world. Letting that coil tighten just to the point of explosion was the most organic thing between them.

"Come for me, Skye," he whispered, ragged and husky.

That tipped them both over the cliff of pure primal pleasure. He growled in the crux of her neck as he poured out his seed. His grip tightened on her ass cheeks.

She called out his name, her mouth falling open to take in a breath. The whole world shuddered around her, and the coil sprung loose. The climax reverberated through her entire body down to her toes. Her muscles greedily contracted around his thick cock, milking him of every drop. He wrapped his arms around her and slowly took them to the floor.

She laid her head on his chest, the room spinning around her. Hearing the beat of his strong heart recentered her world. Grounding her to this spot, to this man, in the most natural rhythm between two people. He was still inside her, their bodies covered in blissful sweat. She never wanted that connection to end.

"That's what I call churning butter," he whispered.

She let out a single laugh because that's all her lungs would allow.

"You came hard." He brushed back the hair from her forehead.

She lifted her head to meet his gaze. "Maybe. You clearly needed that as much as I did."

The corner of his lip curled upward. "I won't deny that. *Maybe* you like the idea that someone might see us."

Oh, God, did she? She swatted his pec. "*Maybe* you're delusional."

"Keep telling yourself that, pumpkin."

She turned her head to hide the blush in her cheeks. Did she like the idea of being watched? Something like this never occurred to her before.

But *before* didn't matter anymore. Guy was in her life now, and just maybe, she liked it.

She bit on her lips to hide her grin and basked in the arms of a man who only wanted to bring pleasure. "Ready for dinner?"

CHAPTER 13

THE SEATTLE COFFEE shop bustled with dozens of patrons on a Wednesday evening. Much more than Reed was expecting. But he needed to finish this search. He was so damn close to discovering the truth about his partner's killer, he could almost taste the moment of sweet justice. Maybe it was the awesome sex with Skye that reinvigorated his drive to push forward. He'd been depleted from a full day working in seclusion, he needed to recharge. Refill his cup, so to speak. Boy, did she overfill it, and then some. Only for him to need more of it. She'd made him so damn hungry.

He chose a different coffee shop this time. Just in case someone was watching, they couldn't form any patterns from his behavior. He wore fake reading glasses and a set of false sideburns. He'd let his facial scruff grow out longer over the last few days to help disguise him from cameras, not to mention sporting a different baseball hat. His baggy windbreaker fit in well with the college crowd, and he tucked himself into the corner to boot up his laptop. It took vulturing that spot for fifteen minutes waiting for the previous customers to clear so he could ensure a semiprivate table.

Piggy-backing off someone else's wifi again, he quickly went down the list of D. Huerta's. He'd rule out as many as he could by narrowing them down to those with some kind of technology background. Degrees, work history, internships, even those related to someone in a digital field. Needless to say, it took a long time. He'd been there several hours, and his ass grew numb on that wooden chair. He ordered a third cup of coffee, paid with cash, and offered the alias "Lars." After burning his tongue on the first sip, he set the cup down without the lid, letting it cool off a bit. He'd lost count of how many names he'd gone through.

The next name came up, Danny Huerta. A graduate of Cal-Tech, along with an internship at a prominent tech company. That was promising. Reed dug a little further and couldn't find anything for the last five years. No employment history, tax documents, or a last known address.

Reed looked up Danny's old Cal-Tech files and easily broke into the university database. It didn't take long for him to come across a graduate photo.

The dark eyes devoid of emotion glared back at him on the screen.

Reed's heart iced over.

He recognized that calculating face from the warehouse. In the picture, he wasn't smiling. Just a determined stare that reminded Reed of countless mugshots, only in a black gown and cap.

"That's him," he muttered.

Finally, he'd found the face that matched the digital footprint. Now he had a name to go with Joe's killer. Not only was this bastard a stone-cold murderer, but an educated one. An American citizen with ridiculous coding and development skills. Danny wasn't just a cartel thug with an appetite for brutality. He had the markings of a true strategizer, perhaps close to the highest level of cartel leadership.

But how did the cartel recruit someone like Huerta?

Reed's fingers practically flew across the keyboard, pulling up all the information he could find on Danny Huerta, and any alias or nickname he could think of. This would be a much longer night, but the glimmer of hope had burst into a righteous fireball that practically lit up the entire atmosphere of his case.

"Now, to catch this cyberpunk."

Something moved in front of him, standing just outside his view.

He glanced up, thinking it was someone possibly asking to use the empty chair beside him. The scrawny man appeared about thirty years old with skinny jeans and old-school brown loafers with no socks. His less-than-polite grimace matched his overly long, mud-colored sweater that was just a bit too tight around the midsection. "Dude, you've been taking up this space for several hours now. D'ya mind moving along to let someone else have a table?"

Reed raised his eyebrows. The last thing he wanted to do was to draw attention to himself. But this was a first. "Are you an employee here?"

"No, my friends and I need a place to sit."

He cocked his head. "So, you've been here all this time watching me? That's creepy."

He sighed, crossing his arms over his deflated chest. "Come on, man. Don't be a squatter."

Reed peered behind the man, where two other bohemian-yuppies eyed him as they poured extra sugar and cinnamon into their massive cups of whip-cream. A messenger bag draped over the shoulder of one of them, with a Vans logo embroidered on the front. Not to mention, an honest-to-God wrist-coil bracelet with a bike-lock key dangling from it. No doubt, it went to the Soma bicycle latched to the tree out in front of the coffee shop.

How he really wanted to put these folks in their place. But he had to keep a low profile. Causing a ruckus would only draw more eyes to him. His disguise wasn't that great, itchy sideburns and all, and someone might figure out he was trying to hide something. Which would only have him end up in the manager's office with the police en route.

Dammit. I was so close to the finish line.

Begrudgingly, he shut his laptop and slid it into its case. When he stood and stared into the ass's smug face, he adjusted his glasses using only his middle finger. "You're welcome."

The drive back to Cascade Creek left him a little deflated. He couldn't figure out why the pit of his stomach was screaming at him. Something was off. Why did it feel like he'd just screwed up somehow? He should be bouncing off the seat, pumping to the music as loud as the dilapidated speakers could handle. He had the single-most prominent lead of the entire case. Joe's killer had a name. With only a few more searches, he could pinpoint the monster's location.

When the sucker was apprehended, Reed could then clear his name and come out of hiding for good. Have his career reinstated. Perhaps even continue a relationship with Skye.

Skye.

Just thinking her name made him smile.

If he ever cleared his name, she'd know the truth. His real identity. Then be furious that he'd lied, and may not ever want to see him again. His spirits dimmed, and the high of identifying Joe's killer fizzled.

No, he shook himself out of those thoughts. She'd look past the deception and realize it was for his safety, and for true justice. She'd see that. He'd convince her, somehow. But only if Danny Huerta was apprehended.

As if the universe read his thoughts, Skye's name flashed across his phone. He answered. "Hey, sunshine."

"Hey, you. Guess what? I don't have class tomorrow night. Wanna have dinner?"

Fuck yes! "Love to. I love your cooking."

She chuckled. "Great. See you at work. Good night."

"'Night."

He had another date with Skye. That was something to look forward to. At least one good thing came out of all this agonizing and tumultuous lifestyle.

Thursday at work, Skye found herself distracted. The never-ending shift thwarted her plans to take Guy on a picnic in the most-perfect spot up in the mountains. Customers had streamed in all morning and hadn't slowed through lunch. The new week's specials were the most popular after the festival. She'd lost track of how many pies she'd baked, they were flying off the shelf faster than she could pull them out of the oven. At least business was back to booming—thanks to Guy's culinary skills—which meant she and the other employees would get their bonuses later in the year. But only if she could focus enough and stop screwing up people's orders or delivering plates to the wrong tables.

"Sunshine," Guy called from the back kitchen.

She spun around as he pointed to the platters of food

sitting under the hot lamps, his eyebrows raised.

"Sorry."

He grinned as she lifted the first plate and balanced it on her forearm. He leaned close.

"You seem to have trouble focusing. Do I need to give you a spanking?" he whispered.

Her eyes widened. *Oh crap!* She licked her lips and managed to shake her head a few times.

He chuckled and turned back to the grill.

Heat flushed her cheeks that had nothing to do with the warming lamps for the food. If anyone looked closely, they might assume she was feverish. She was both appalled and excited about the prospect of Guy spanking her.

Why? How crazy is that? Who in their right mind wants a spanking?

Well, if not her, then why was her heart racing?

She set the plates down with an obligatory smile and turned to cool her cheeks with the back of her hands. Guy could turn her insides to mush with nothing more than a few words.

God, help me get through the day.

Reed arrived at Skye's door at five o'clock as she'd requested. She was concerned about the sun setting, which told him she had plans for them outside.

The door swung open. Her face was as bright and pink as during their shift. "Great. You're here."

He chuckled. "Where else would I be?"

She wore a pair of faded blue jeans, a pink sweater, and her camel-colored jacket. She tucked her hair behind her right ear, and asked, "Help me carry this stuff, okay?"

He strode behind her to the kitchen. A basket and a canvas bag sat on the island.

"A picnic?" he asked. He honestly couldn't remember the last time he'd been on an outdoor picnic. "Where to?"

"You'll see." She beamed.

"Look at you, all proud of yourself for surprising me."

"You excited?" she asked.

"Of course. Anywhere with you excites me.

Her grin widened, and she handed him the basket. "Can you carry these? I'll grab the blankets."

After the truck was loaded, he followed her directions along a road, leading away from town. They wove around the side of a mountain and higher in elevation. A few turns later, they plateaued to a clearing about a hundred yards that stretched along a crystal-clear lake.

Reed stepped out of the truck. "Holy mother. This is spectacular."

"Isn't it?" Skye grinned at him. "Best secret ever."

No shit! This state was growing on him more and more every flippin' day. If he ever had to get up and leave, it might just break his heart.

He helped heft the food from the truck and set it at the end of the blanket she'd laid on the ground.

Skye made quick work of unpacking. "Can you open the wine?"

He reached for the corkscrew. "What are we havin'?"

"Diced roasted chicken, a few different cheeses, a baguette, veggies with ranch dip, and fruit. Stuff we can eat with our fingers. Plated food doesn't work as well out here."

"Good thinking." He handed her a clear plastic glass of wine. "Cheers."

Here he was again, living a normal life. Everything on the surface looked positively common. He never knew how much he craved a simple life like this. Would he ever have this consistently? Could he ever have the wife and kids and go on picnics like this again? That is, without having to constantly look over his shoulder.

"I'm going out on a precarious limb here to ask you a very personal question." Skye's smile turned determined.

"Oh, boy." He popped a piece of chicken into his mouth.

"Where do you see this going?"

"See what?"

"Us."

He slowed his chewing. "You mean tonight?"

"Tonight, tomorrow, and beyond."

His heart rate kicked up. He just kept watching her, hoping his mind would come up with something neutral enough to keep her happy, without sacrificing his cover.

"Does that question scare you?" she asked, casually leaning back on her elbow, like throwing a fast curveball at a guy who was merely a passing fancy.

"From you, no. Which is the scary part."

Her smile slipped. "What does that mean?"

The truth was the only thing he could think of. "I never allowed myself to hope a woman as gorgeous, vibrant, and caring as you would be interested in me. So, I've just been enjoying the time we have together, for however long it lasts."

She paused, poking a cheese cube with a toothpick. "Are you saying I'm a fling to you?"

He was ashamed to admit that at the very beginning, yes, that's what she was to him. Because he couldn't dare try for anything more permanent. Now, he didn't want her to be a fling. It was the last thing she was to him.

On a deep breath, he took her hand and interlaced her fingers with his. "You are not a fling. You're a taste of heaven. A reminder that you are exactly the kind of woman a guy like me would want to spend forever with. But I'm also cautious of it."

"Why? Do I bore you?"

The corner of his mouth lifted. "Boring is never a word that describes you. The furthest thing from it."

"This whole town can be boring sometimes, but that doesn't make me a fleeting dalliance either." Her voice had a defensive edge. "I'm not asking for a diamond ring if that's what you're inferring. But I want to make sure that the possibility is somewhere in your mind down the road."

He tended closer, placing a simple, slow kiss on her lips. "The possibility is definitely in my mind."

The twinkle in her eye and the glowing smile on her lips told him he chose the right words.

Words that, to him, were not a lie. If he didn't have this goddamn cloud hanging over his head, planning the rest of his life with this woman would be the top of his list. Hell, his entire list. He didn't need to "date" anyone else to know this was the woman for him.

Skye cleared her throat. "Ok, dig in."

"How many times have you been here?" he asked.

She finished her bite of bread. "About five, I think. I found it accidentally when I was supposed to meet a study group. I completely missed the meeting, but found this instead."

"Good find."

"Just wait until you see the sunset."

He would try and look at her promising sunset view, but really he had some other ideas. Being alone with Skye here in this picturesque place worthy of nature calendars brought ideas into his head that, if spoken allowed, might get him slapped.

They ate a few more bites, chatted about her degree,

and some residents that frequented the diner. The bottle of wine was nearly empty.

"Oh, look." She pointed west to a deep-V created in the mountain range. The sun glowed a golden yellow while the sky turned a brilliant orange.

"So, have you ever brought one of your boyfriends up here?"

"No. I didn't have a lot of boyfriends, Guy."

"No?" He intentionally tilted his head as he furrowed his brows and took her wine glass, setting it behind him. "Well, it would be terrible to have this," he lifted his arm toward the setting sun, "go to waste. Don't you agree?"

A blush crept over her cheeks, the pink mimicking the hue of the sky. "What are you talking about?"

He pulled her closer and stroked her abdomen as he leaned in for a kiss. "I'm talking about being one with nature."

"Guy," she whispered over his mouth, "there are still houses around here."

He knew what was around; he'd scoped the area on the ride up and as they set up. The closest houses were buried in a ton of evergreens, a football field away. "So? They won't care." He laced kisses on her neck, pulling at her jacket and sweater to gain more access. Her pulse thumped under his lips.

"What if I care?" she said between sweet little breaths.

"Do you?" His hand slipped under her sweater to her warm, silky skin. "I mean, they may or may not see you, but if I'm giving you one of the best orgasms you've ever had, would it matter?"

Her breath hitched softly.

"With darkness closing in on us, no one would be able to see anyway. Only if you screamed my name..."

"I don't know, Guy." Her words came out breathy.

"I'll tell you what. Let's make out a little. Pretend we're in high school, trying out new things with each other. If you want to stop, we stop. That simple." Hopefully he could convince her otherwise once she started warming up.

She bit her lower lip playfully, looking so delectable he could barely hold himself back. "Were you a bad boy in high school?"

His grin widened. "If you were in my class, I certainly would've been."

She giggled. "What would a nervous teenager do in a moment like this?"

"Lie back."

As she lay on the blanket, Reed pushed aside the food containers, then positioned himself over her.

She smiled under him, her hair spread out around her head on the blanket. He twirled a few strands around his fingers, and let the apple-scented shampoo linger up to his face. She sighed when he returned to kissing her neck, pulling on her sweater's neckline. She moaned as he slipped a hand under the soft fabric and danced his fingertips over her stomach.

The hem of her sweater rose. He distracted her with kisses trailing up her neck, her jaw, to her lips, diving in with a emmence longing. He pushed the garment higher, revealing her lace-covered breasts. His lips quickly laid claim to a nipple peaking underneath. She moaned but didn't say a word. He worked her other nipple between his thumb and forefinger. After a few beats, he switched—his mouth laving and sucking one nipple and fingers on the other.

She squirmed beneath him, those beautiful mewls of pleasure urging him on.

Wordlessly, he grabbed the second blanket and unfolded it. Without objection, she allowed him to help her out of her jacket and sweater, then quickly covered them with a blanket tent.

His dick surged behind his jeans, starting to feel uncomfortable.

Her hand tunneled between them and cupped his raging erection.

"Fuck, Skye. What I wouldn't give to have your hands on me."

She paused a fraction of a second, deliberating. Then, she eased open his fly and reached for him under his briefs.

Searing heat surged his body.

Gee-zus!

She stroked him slowly, and he unwittingly groaned into her mouth.

In a brave move, he pulled down her bra straps, revealing her delicious tits. He broke the kiss and sucked in a hard nub, roaming his tongue freely over her sweet skin.

She controlled her moans, stifling the sound to prevent anyone from hearing. But no one would, not out here. He was certain of it.

Balancing his weight on one elbow, he focused on her pants, loosening enough to make room for his hand. Watching her face, he slipped his fingers under her lace panties, sliding a digit through her slit.

"Ah."

"You feel incredible, Skye." Her wetness coated his finger and the back of his hand from her panties. He could drive into her this instant, but she had to want it, too. To want to be taken outside like this.

He couldn't say why, but he wanted her naked. Out here, just for him. Feeling only him pleasuring her, thinking about only him and how good they felt together. How connected they were. Even if they couldn't have forever, they could have now. No barriers between them.

And he didn't give a flying fuck if anyone watched. This was his woman. He would show her how sweet it was to indulge in unadulterated pleasure, giving herself over completely to the sensation.

His mouth lapped and suckled her breasts as he gently tugged at her garments, making more room.

"Guy," she whispered.

He glanced in her eyes, but her protests were weak. His mouth trailed down her torso, dipping his tongue into her navel. "Let me taste you, Skye. We have the blanket to cover you."

The blanket would shield them, but frankly, in another few minutes, the sunlight would disappear completely. The moon and stars already flickered in the open sky.

She nodded.

That was all he needed. He lifted and grabbed her waistband, panties too, and dragged them off her legs. Her head darted left and right.

He yanked the blanket over him and crouched down between her legs, his hand lifting her hips to his mouth.

He loved her smell. The musky, intoxicating scent of her sex better than any drug. He lapped at her pussy and clit like it was a sweet, ripe fruit ready to drip everywhere.

She moaned and panted. "Guy."

He groaned and suckled her clit, increasing the pressure.

Her little shriek coupled with a tightened grip on his hair.

Oh, that sweet combination stretched his dick another inch against his zipper. He would relish making her come out here. Maybe twice.

He lifted his torso and returned to her lips. He tangled with her tongue, diving as deep as he could. A desperate, needy kiss that hinted of the urgency of lovemaking still to come. "Push down my pants, baby. If you're a little naked, I should be too."

She grinned, her blue eyes looking nearly black in the night. Her flushed face, all pink from arousal, turned him on so bad. She reached for his jeans and briefs, pushing them beyond his ass.

Close enough.

He slid back and pushed her legs wide, hearing the clank of containers behind him. He ate at her, cherishing her moans and wiggles under his attention. He reached back and fished out a rubber from his pants pocket.

He drove two fingers into her wet channel, curling into her sweet spot.

Her body twitched, and a gasp escaped her lips. She covered her mouth with the edge of the blanket, muffling the moans. She was incredibly close.

He stretched up his arms under her back, unhooking her bra. He flung it to the side, pulling back some blanket in the process. He cupped her breasts while his mouth made love to her pussy.

Her hips lifted, grinding against his face. A surge of liquid heat filled his mouth, signaling she'd tipped over the edge.

He twisted her nipples and pressed harder against her clit, letting her writhe and moan through her orgasm, panting out his name.

When she was done, her cheeks so red and that hazy, drunken look on her face so exquisite, he rose and whipped off his shirt. The blanket fell behind him, and he didn't pull it back. Instead, he laid his body against hers, chest to chest, and let his cock wedge at her entrance.

"Do you want me to stop?" *Please don't say yes.* He'd never been harder in his life. The ache was almost painful; he needed inside her so badly.

"You're crazy. You know that, right?" She grinned.

"I want to hear you, sweetheart. It's dark now. No one can see us. Make all the noises you want. I want to hear you come again."

She glanced around again, then nodded.

Thank God.

He pushed into her, full to the hilt.

Her pussy was so damn hot, so tight, he swore he'd just slid into heaven. He couldn't hold back his moan. Her sweet voice mingled with his in the sexiest moan in the Cascades.

"God, Guy. You feel so good."

He thought the same thing about her, but the words were stuck behind a lustful haze. He didn't dare speak until he was sure he wouldn't explode right then. He could still taste her on his tongue, that tangy sweetness of her nectar.

"Mm," she hummed, her hips rocking into him.

He grabbed the blanket and bunched it under her ass, changing the angle. With a slow pump at first, he increased the pace with every thrust.

"Ah."

He then grasped her hands above her head, lacing their fingers together. "Wrap your legs around me, sweetheart."

She did, hooking her ankles together behind his ass.

He pumped steadily, holding back his own climax until she was ready. His whole body shook, and hot sweat dripped down the back of his neck as he strained to keep from exploding. The darkness settled around them, but her creamy skin and flushed cheeks were still visible in the moonlight. He arched his back, scanning her body, watching their joining. "You're beautiful, Skye. Breathtaking."

He increased his thrusts, adding more power and speed.

"Unh," she breathed. She pressed her lips closed, stifling her moan.

"No, baby. Let it out. Let me hear you." He thrust again.

"Ah," she called out louder.

Her breasts bounced with their lustful rhythm.

He could barely hold back, and he dug his toes into the blanket.

Her eyes widened. "Oh. Don't stop. Please, don't stop."

He claimed her mouth while pumping into her, then pulled back, eager to hear her cries of pleasure.

Her eyes pinched closed, her mouth gaped, and she bowed her back.

"Ah, Guy," she cried the sound echoing off the treeline. Her muscles tightened around his cock.

His tempo faltered, hearing the wrong name in that moment. But her sweet body squeezed around his dick in the hottest, searing vise, making him forget to feel guilty. He released his own built-up tension. Fireworks exploded from his groin out, radiating to every cell in his body.

He collapsed, bracing his weight on one forearm, panting into her shoulder.

"How did you do that?" she panted out.

"Do what?" He lifted to meet her gaze.

"Get me completely naked out here."

"Baby, I didn't get you to do anything. We did it."

"Ha," she barked out. "You really are a secret bad boy. If only I'd known you back in high school."

He yanked up the blanket to cover them against the chill in the air, then kissed her sweetly. "You bring it out of me. I love breaking the rules with you."

Her face turned placid.

"We are explosive together, sweetheart. I want it to feel that way every time we're together."

He wrapped her close, laying skin-to-skin, gazing at the stars above. His mind wandered to the idea of what if he *had* known her back in high school. He was a total computer nerd back then. Completely introverted and focused on having fun and causing havoc behind the screen. Blonde bombshell she was, no doubt she wouldn't have given him a passing glance, let alone be interested in these kinds of sexual interludes with him.

But damn, she would've been tempting. Perhaps enough of a reason for him to step out of his digital, black-hat world and try a *normal* adolescence for a change.

But then again, if he'd done that, he would've never been recruited by Joe in the first place. Which meant he would've never joined the DEA as a cybersecurity expert, exchanging the black hat for a white one. Joe might never have died if it weren't for Reed screwing with the cartel's money. Ultimately, he never would've met Skye.

The sequences of his life choices that led to this moment blew his mind.

"Wow," he muttered aloud.

"I know," Skye answered.

He squeezed her tighter against his side. Damn, he wanted this. Every single day. Every morning waking up to this face. This feel of her soft body against his. But he'd already screwed it up. The whole time she kept using his alias. He cringed inside each time he heard it. He wanted her to say his real name. Which meant if he ever divulged the truth, she would run. Faster than a flash boil.

Shit.

This relationship was already doomed. Just as he started to care for her so deeply, it actually *hurt* inside. Unless he could salvage it somehow. When he told her the truth, he had to show her that his one lie was for a greater good. Getting this vicious cartel scum behind bars. Actually, return to Skye as a DEA hero, even though the very idea of white knights had previously irritated him.

There was more than one way to be a hero.

Maybe he could convince her to forgive him for the few lies he *had* to tell to avenge Joe's death.

Which meant he had to catch the fucker first.

He kissed the side of her head, savoring this sweet moment for a little longer. He'd continue his hunt in the morning. For now, he wanted to imprint this feeling in his memory. Hold her for just a while longer.

CHAPTER 14

SKYE'S TEDIOUS COMMUNICATIONS class was so much more bearable with images of the picnic with Guy fluttering through her mind the whole ninety minutes. She'd actually caught herself sighing with pleasure several times during the lecture. Truly on Cloud Nine.

Her shift that morning was just as delicious, with her and Guy stealing secret kisses in the back. When it was time for her to head to class, she desperately just wanted to skip. Spend the rest of the day and into the evening in his bed. But he'd urged her to go to class instead.

"I have work to do too. Go ace your tests, and we'll celebrate after."

She wasn't sure what work he referred to, but she surmised it was housework or learning new recipes.

Finally, her professor finished his lesson, and she scooped up her things to rush out. The twilight sky filled her with warmth despite the crisp breeze as she walked to her car. Normally, she'd head home to make herself a boring dinner, or sometimes spend the evening studying at Lynée's. But she had half a mind to grab some food on the way back and surprise Guy with dinner in bed. She'd have to text him and find out where he lived. She pulled out her phone.

"Hi, gorgeous."

Skye looked up at the figure beside her car. She gasped.

Vance.

Her heart hardened in her chest.

He flashed his too-handsome-for-his-own-good smile. The same one she'd fallen for all those years ago. But she was much smarter this time around.

"What are you doing here?" she asked. Making sure to keep distance between them.

"Came to see you."

"How did you know I was here?"

"I wanted to apologize." He shoved his hands in his hoodie's pockets. Then stepped closer.

Skye stepped back and gripped her keys tighter.

Vance actually winced. Then stopped. "Back at the festival, I came off as pushy and threatening. That's not what I intended. The new guy you were with put me on my guard. I honestly don't want any hard feelings between us."

The tightness in her chest eased. She lowered her defenses a little. At least he was acknowledging his behavior. "That's good to hear. I'd rather just forget about all that."

He sighed through a grateful smile. "You look great, by the way. Really happy."

"I am."

"Finishing up your degree? You're close to your last credits, right?"

She pressed her lips together. "No. I still had a few years left. But I was derailed by a hospital stay, thanks to you."

He lost his smile, and his brows pulled together. "That's another thing I wanted to apologize for. I had some control issues back then. Led to a lot of anger."

"Which you took out on me."

"I know. I'm sorry. Much of that was because of my dad. He put a lot of pressure on me."

Skye narrowed her eyes. She wasn't sure where he was going with this. He wasn't even enrolled in college at the time, so whatever pressure his fancy attorney-father had put on him had nothing to do with her. "Well, I hope you got that all worked out with him. I need to get going."

She wanted to step toward her car, but Vance stood firmly between her and escape.

"Actually, I'm seeing a therapist now. The interaction between you and I back then made me realize I needed some help."

"That's good, Vance."

"I'm better now. I really think you'd be impressed." He stepped closer.

Skye raised her hand. "I'm happy for you. And for whatever girl you end up with, I hope she has a better experience than I did. I need to go."

"That's just it." He smiled at her again, that smooth, charming grin meant to knock her on her ass. "I want you to be that girl. Let's give us a try again."

The prickle that raced up her spine, raising the hairs on her neck, landed squarely on the scar on her left shoulder. The pain from that tumble down the stairs re-emerged throughout her whole body. Reminding her in vivid detail why that snake-like smile was a ploy. He hadn't changed at all.

But for some reason, her feet wouldn't budge. It was as if her entire body had frozen in place.

He stepped closer. He was so much taller than her, he had a way of making her feel like a helpless rabbit. His hand reached out to grab her elbow and gently pulled her in.

"We were meant to be together," he muttered softly. "After everything we've been through, you were always mine." He ducked his head to kiss her.

That tug on her arm with his last words snapped her out of her prey-state. She ground her feet to the pavement and grabbed his hand. In one quick jerk, she bent his hand back, nearly breaking his fingers. Then she yanked it down hard.

Vance howled.

She spun around him to keep his torso away from her but kept his arm and hand bent awkwardly behind his back.

A move from the self-defense course came back like muscle memory. Lynée had been right urging her to take it.

Vance tried to jerk free, but she held him immobilized in that grip.

"Let me make this very clear." She ground her feet to the pavement, refusing to budge to this bully. "You and I are through. There is *zero* chance of us getting back together. This is not a signal for you to try harder; this means *no*."

She tugged on his hand harder, feeling a few knuckles pop. He yelped.

"When I let go, you're going to walk away and never look for me again."

"Let go, bitch!"

There's the Vance I know.

Back in college, she might've fallen for that lost puppy routine. But not now.

He tried to tug out of her grasp again.

She shoved him forward to put more distance between them. He stumbled and landed on his knees. But quickly scrambled to his feet.

The rage in his eyes as he came toward her set her

mind back into panic. What else could she remember from that course? How far was he going to take this?

Chatter carried on the breeze behind her. Skye turned to a group of three students walking toward their cars. When they spotted the pair of them and the interaction, they moved her way.

"Hey," one guy called. "Are you okay?"

Skye looked back at Vance, whose menacing stance eased off a little. "She's fine. Mind your business."

The trio came closer, the two guys she recognized from her class, but didn't know their names. They gave her ex-boyfriend a doubtful look.

He rubbed his fingers and fisted his hand by his side. His glare all for Skye.

"I was just telling Vance here to go away and leave me alone." She lifted her chin, finding more strength in her voice. "He was leaving, weren't you, *Vance*?"

One of her classmates picked up on her obvious message. Then stood beside her. "You heard her, buddy."

"Stay out of this," he shot back. "This is between her and me."

"She made it really clear," he returned, "she doesn't want to see you again."

"Don't mess with me," Vance shot back. "I'm more connected than your small, podunk-brain can imagine. I can have your life crumpled up into cobwebs by next week."

"This isn't Seattle." Skye stepped forward. "Your father has no reach out here. Save yourself more embarrassment and just drive away."

His glare turned vicious and threatening, and he took a step forward. "This isn't over, bitch."

Skye didn't budge an inch, just glared right back. "Yes, it is. You are never to speak to me again. We. Are. Through.

Are we clear?"

Her classmate took a picture of Vance and smiled. "Now that we know your name and have taken your photo, I suggest you leave and don't come back. If she has so much as a busted taillight or a creepy text," waving his phone in the air, "you're the primary suspect."

Vance shoved his fists back in his pockets. He eyed the group, then looked back at her. "We are so through, whore."

She almost chuckled at that. His last lash was as pathetic as his twisted mind. She and her classmates stood there and watched him storm off and get back in his car. A classmate shot one last photo of his license plate number before Vance peeled out of the parking lot.

"Wow, he's a real charmer." Her classmate shook his head. "The wrist lock you gave him was stellar. Saw it all the way from the sidewalk. Well done."

She smiled. "Thanks." The adrenaline pumping through her veins was too much, and she just started laughing. "Hell, that was a long time coming."

"How does it feel?" he asked, smiling right along with her. "Putting that bully in his place?"

"Damn good."

That asshole had no control over her anymore. She wanted to celebrate her revelation. In finally taking back her power.

She licked her lips. She was in the process of texting Guy. If she told him about Vance, what would he do?

Maybe better to tell him in person. But she had to tell someone. The relief, the empowerment, sent her adrenaline into overdrive.

God, it feels so good to tell that asshole off. To be done with him once and for all.

Her car partially drove itself. She'd tell Guy tomorrow,

but tonight she'd celebrate with Lynée.

CHAPTER 15

THE FIRST CUSTOMERS walked into the diner, the familiar jingle sounding over the door. But there was still no sign of Guy.

Skye couldn't wait to tell him about her "run-in" with Vance. He'd be pissed at first, but she knew in her gut he'd be proud of the way she stood up to the jerk.

She might have to spend the next hour convincing him not to go beat up the a-hole, but that was to be expected—she smiled to herself—and accepted.

Her watch read six-thirty. Still no Guy. Skye glanced back at the kitchen. Ralph had jumped on the grill to get things started. He shot her a frustrated look.

"Where the hell is he?" her boss grumbled.

"He's never been late before. Do you think he's okay?"

"At this point, he better not be."

As she served the first set of regulars, Skye's imagination whirled. Each possibility for an explanation as to why Guy was MIA this morning was as unlikely as the next. Like in a car wreck, lying unconscious in a ditch somewhere, or arrested for putting his hands on Vance at the festival. Or worse, Vance retaliated on her by going after the guy who made him look like a complete ass.

She forced herself into more reasonable explanations,

such as a flat tire, woke up sick and forgot to call, or got drunk watching a *Live PD* rerun the previous evening and is still passed out. Did he even watch that show? She assumed he was former law enforcement from their conversation about his partner getting shot in the line of duty.

"Probably just slept through his alarm," she muttered to herself as she started another pot of coffee. Then she ducked behind the counter to call him.

Straight to voicemail. And not his own voice, but the robo-voice. Which was strange to her. Why wouldn't someone want to use their own voicemail message? Unless he really was on the run, and he used one of those fake burner phones.

She snorted.

Ralph squeezed past her with a bin of chopped potatoes. "I'm gonna kill him. The second he walks through that door, I'll put a salt shaker up his ass."

"Easy, boss-man. Do you think I should call Wyatt to go check on him?"

He poured the potatoes into a pot on the stove. "Don't bother the sheriff with little stuff like this. He's got enough to do than check on a slacker."

Wow, could her boss overreact. They both knew Guy was no slacker. His cooking had single-handedly revitalized this diner.

Skye stared at Guy's contact number on her phone screen. Her stomach grew unsettled. Something was wrong.

After the shit with Vance showing up the prior night, this was just too coincidental.

She dashed back to the office and perused Ralph's files for Guy's application to get his home address. Since she was the one who handled all the tax forms for the diner, it wasn't that big of a deal. Ralph had given her access. But she had no idea when she'd be able to sneak away and check on their missing cook.

Skye held the paper in her hand, a loud *hiss* from the kitchen sizzling in the air as her boss started frying potatoes. Maybe she was overreacting. Perhaps Ralph was right, and Guy was slacking off today. But everything she knew about him didn't match up to skipping work.

She typed his address into her phone contact. Then she returned to the floor to serve her customers.

The door chimed again.

Her head shot up, hoping it was Guy.

Nayanna strolled in, already in her apron, and her black hair pulled back for her shift. She smiled at Skye. "Mornin'."

Skye's heart sank. Her nerves amped up again.

With a glance at the clock, she shoved her phone in her pocket. "I hate to ask this of you right as you walk in, but can you cover the tables for a little bit? I'll be right back."

"Sure. Everything okay?" Nayanna tied the apron around her waist.

"It's probably nothing." She untied her own apron and grabbed her keys from under the counter. "But if I don't check..."

Nayanna sighed. "Yeah, it'll eat at your brain like the walking dead. Hurry back."

"Hopefully, with our cook in a fishing net."

The last thing she saw was a strange expression on Nayanna's face before the diner's door closed behind her.

Skye rolled up the long gravel drive of Guy's cabin. After several twists and bends up the long hill, the cabin came into view. Small and quaint against the towering pines around it with a great view of a mountain peak through the treetops. Cozy was the first word that came to mind as she stared at it. Would probably be gorgeous in winter. She could actually imagine the lights on inside, with smoke billowing from the chimney with a warm and comfortable fire inside, the whole thing blanketed by snow in the twilight. The kind of image one would expect on a Christmas card. She'd lived in Cascade Creek her whole life and had never seen this cabin.

Guy's truck was parked right in front. At least she knew he was home.

She stepped out of her car and slammed the door. The only sound in this part of the mountains, other than the gravel crunching under her boots, was the trickling stream a few hundred yards away. The same stream wound its way to the south side of town into the creek that fed into a Snoqualmie River tributary. Everyone around here knew that sound like their own heartbeat.

Several loud thumps came from inside the cabin. Like something dropped on the hardwood floors.

Guy must be moving furniture around.

Jerk. Standing up the diner to redecorate.

Only a few paces later, the thumps were replaced with a loud *bang*.

Skye froze.

A gunshot. She knew that sound well enough, too. This was a hunting area. But why in the world would—

Two more loud *bangs* ripped through the air.

Skye ducked behind Guy's truck on instinct.

As she looked over the back-bed, the front door burst open. The force splintered the wood, and planks flew off the hinges. A man charged across the porch and down the stairs.

Not Guy.

This man looked older, sweat-soaked salt-and-pepper

hair in a Seahawk green hoodie and gray pants covered in mud. Grasped in his hand was a black pistol.

Skye's feet wouldn't move. She was nailed to the spot, her whole body frozen. The man came closer to her. Each step in slow motion, the space between heartbeats pounding in her ears dragged out in time with his footsteps. Like a horror movie where the gory end of the hero's life is captured frame by frame in vivid detail, but the audience is too slow to stop it from happening.

His wild gaze landed on her.

Her gasp lodged in her throat.

The man's arm rose slowly. His face blurred as she focused on the dark end of that pistol.

Boom!

Skye flinched.

Smoke spiraled from the end of the man's gun.

She waited for the pain.

The man turned but took off in the opposite direction. He fired more shots behind him as he ran.

Another large *boom* came from the other side of the house.

Skye's gaze shifted.

Guy crouched against the side of the cabin, aiming a shotgun at the man.

Boom!

A shell slammed into the intruder's back, red splatter bursting through his chest. He fell hard into gravel, skidding across the rocks. When he stopped, he didn't move. Blood oozed out of his chest and started to pool over the rocks.

"Skye!" Guy darted across the driveway, his gaze fixed on the front door.

She took a step back, her body moving on its own will to getaway.

He was like a beast, barreling toward her with a hard, cold look on him. The look of a killer.

That wasn't *her* Guy.

But she still couldn't command her legs to move faster. The only thing she could muster was to finally inhale.

Guy blew past her, grabbing her elbow as he went, and yanked her down.

She opened her mouth to scream.

He wrapped his arm around her neck and smothered her mouth. Her scream never made it past the palm of his hand. He crouched them both behind the front tire of his truck.

"There's one more," he whispered.

Her spine turned cold as if doused with a bucket of snow.

He released his hand and rose to look through the window.

Gunshots fired, the bullets plinking into the other side of his truck.

He ducked down again.

She covered her own mouth to keep herself from making noise. Because she didn't trust her mind to comply.

The man standing beside her was not the same one she'd become infatuated with at the diner, had fallen completely in love with. *That* Guy had been endearing, funny, and entertaining. Not to mention calm and collected. *This* Guy was detached, calculating, and thoroughly intimidating.

"Are you hurt?" he whispered.

She only now registered his black and blue flannel shirt and old jeans. And bare feet. His hair was wet as if he'd recently gotten out of the shower.

"Are you hurt?" he repeated, harsher.

She looked down at herself. No blood, no guts ripped out, though she wasn't sure what to expect to see. The other man's gun had certainly fired. Aimed directly at her.

Why couldn't she feel anything?

"I—I don't think so," she whispered back. "What the hell is going on here?"

He didn't answer. Just continued to peek over the truck's hood for the culprit.

"Guy, answer me," Skye hissed.

"Ssh," he replied. "Don't move."

Before she could respond, he darted in front of the truck, his shotgun aimed at the house. He moved fast, his reflexes clearly instinctual, even in bare feet on rough gravel. In only a few quick steps, he was behind the other side of the house.

Panic took over. Crouching behind his truck all by herself with another gunman out there somewhere, where she couldn't see...

Her breathing escalated, and she couldn't focus.

What was the last thing he'd said?

She looked up and spotted her car. Only a dozen paces from where she huddled. She'd be safe in there. Her keys were in her pocket. If she dashed fast enough, she could make it to her door, and drive off before he came back. Her hands fumbled in her pocket.

Gunshots ripped through the air, and then another loud *boom*.

Skye yelped, her keys dropping to the ground. Then she dared to look over the hood.

Another man in a dark green jersey and black pants raced across the side yard, trying to reach the treeline.

Guy darted after him, dropping his shotgun in the process, and pulled a pistol from the back of his waistband.

He fired shot after shot, still bolting after him.

Green-Jersey darted behind a tree, moving from one to the other down the hill toward the road, dodging bullets between the pines.

Guy switched out his clip in half a heartbeat, dropping the empty one on the ground and replacing it with a new one. He fired again and again until his third bullet struck the man in the back.

The assailant fell to his knees, rolled down the hill a few yards, and stopped. He didn't get up.

Guy ran over to him, his pistol aimed at the man's body the whole time. With a cold face, he plugged another bullet in the man's head.

Skye flinched at the sound. Her whole body shook. Her knees gave out, and she dropped to the gravel. Her fingers found her keys, which sparked new energy into her. With a giant shove to her feet, she slowly backed up to her car.

Guy looked over, his expression eerily blank. Hard. Until he noticed she was leaving.

"Skye, wait," he called.

No way in hell. Granted, she was a big fan of suspense stories and high-pounding action, but only when they were on the page. Not in real freakin life. Not when real bullets flew at her, and she got to witness two men get killed right in front of her. This was far beyond her wild imagination, and much too...*real.*

She ran for it. Her car wasn't nearly as close as she'd thought. Her heart pounded in her throat.

Guy's footsteps on the grass were clear as day in her ears.

She reached her car and bungled with the door handle.

Gravel crunched quickly under Guy's steps as he approached, sending her panic into overload. He was so much closer now. The door opened just as he reached her side.

She only had time to turn and see his own panicked expression.

Then he pinned her to the side of the car.

"I won't say anything," she muttered, clamping her eyes shut. She had no idea which words came out of her mouth. Whatever it took to get away from him, get away from the dead bodies, she'd say it. "I swear, I won't tell a soul. I didn't see anything. I was never here."

God, how she willed herself to believe those words.

His rough sigh breathed against her neck. His whole body pressed her against the car, strong and unyielding. But she didn't feel any pain.

"I'm so sorry you had to see that. I can imagine the horrible things you must think of me right now. But I swear to God, I am not the bad guy." His voice shook on the last few words.

She dared to open her eyes.

His dark chocolate irises bored into hers with a desperate plea. His chest rose and fell with each breath. Much like her own. Hers was from fear.

"I will *never* hurt you," he continued. Finally, he backed up. "But you aren't safe out here. We have to go inside." He stuffed his pistol into his back waistband and held out his hand.

She eyed it. Like it was a snake about to strike.

"Who are you?" she asked. Though she wasn't sure she really wanted to know the answer.

"I'll explain everything inside."

"You want me to follow someone who's repeatedly lied and just shot two people like they were target practice."

His expression hardened. "I've never lied to you."

She swallowed hard.

"I had to shoot them. To keep them from killing me," he added. "And you."

Skye hugged herself, keeping as much distance as she could between herself and Guy. His cabin looked clean and organized, despite the few pieces of destroyed furniture where there had clearly been an earlier fight. The acrid stench of gunfire lingered in the air.

He moved quickly through the house, pulling two duffel bags from a closet. He gathered things from various places stashed throughout the rooms. Extra guns, loaded clips, and computer equipment. His face was expressionless. Focused. Like running through a checklist in his head. His silence unnerved her even more than she already was.

There was no way this was about Vance. This was much worse.

"Who are you?" she asked.

He stopped, giving her a resigned look.

"When you said 'partner,' I assumed that meant police." Her whole heart just collapsed in on itself. All her expectations were nothing more than assumptions. False ones. Lies. "You really are a secret agent."

His lips thinned. Then he pulled something out of the inside pocket on the duffel bag. He handed it over.

The old leather wallet was thick. Cold. She opened it to find a shiny gold badge, with an eagle etched on the top. In a bright blue circle were the words U.S. Drug Enforcement Administration, Special Agent.

Her fingers tightened around the badge.

"I've been undercover for three years. Those men outside were from a Mexican cartel. If they found me here, more are coming."

"What do they want with you all the way up here?"

He paused, his expression a little more cautious as if he didn't know if he should tell her. "Last year, they killed my partner. I've been searching for the man responsible, and they're trying to stop me."

Her heartfelt heavy. A hundred more questions came to mind, but she didn't know what to ask first. She sat on the arm of the sofa, still clutching his badge. "Is Guy your real name?"

He sat on the coffee table in front of her, his eyes softening. "That is the one thing I couldn't be honest about. You called me Guy. I ran with it."

Her heart dropped to her stomach. At the same time, he'd ripped the rug from under her love-stricken feet. She forced herself to ask, "What's your real name?"

"Reed. Reed Monroe."

She pressed her lips together. "You don't look like a Reed."

His cheek twitched like he was trying to hide a smile. "What do I look like?"

"Guy."

Shit. She really wanted him to be Guy. Because she'd fallen in love with Guy. Had become addicted to sex with Guy. Could actually see a future with the short-order cook at Rock Road Diner. Once again, her heart had betrayed her. Fallen in love with a man who turned out to be completely different than her expectations.

He cradled her hands in his. His palms were rough but warm. "It's still me, Skye. Same man from the diner, from the festival...from our picnic. Don't pull away."

She swallowed hard. He looked the same...kind of. He was harsher, colder. But who wouldn't be after killing two people?

"Everything I've told you is confidential. You know enough to send me to prison for a long time."

"Why did you tell me?"

He sighed and sat back. Gripping the edge of the coffee table. "I've been on my own for a year. Running from one thug after another, trying to stay alive. I didn't dare involve anyone else because of how brutal these psychos are. Then I met you and had my first kind and genuine interaction with another human being. After all this time. With one as beautiful as you...I didn't want to lose that."

She watched his Adam's apple rise and fall, and the square line of his jaw hardened. She couldn't imagine being alone for that long. To the point where one craved a mere cordial interaction. Anyone else might've turned into a monster, living on nothing but animalistic instinct. Becoming the psychopaths that had chased him. But Guy hadn't. *Reed* hadn't. After all that time on the run, the harsh lifestyle, constant vigilance, and solitude, he was still this charming, funny, and personable man that everyone in town had come to like.

A man she'd fallen in love with.

Or was that all just a ruse? A fake persona to get her into bed? Why not, if he knew he wasn't going to be here that long. Just hiding out long enough until he could lose whatever tail followed him.

"That's why you never wanted your picture taken," she muttered. "The holes in the side of your truck. And why you never brought me back here, instead of always staying at my place."

He didn't respond to that. Hell, he didn't even have the decency to look remorseful or guilty.

The hopeless feeling in her abdomen churned into

fury, over boiling and rising up her throat. Turning everything inside raging hot. And not the fun kind.

"Everything between us wasn't real. You used me. You deceived me because you knew you were going to leave town soon."

Finally, his stoic face changed to one of shock. "Skye, baby…"

"*Don't* call me that. You were just hiding out long enough until you could lose whoever was following you. Why not enjoy a good lay while you're at it?" Her voice rose with every accusation. "Never mind that you've put me in danger too. Why would you care? You won't be here long enough to see the repercussions anyway."

His shock turned to a wounded grimace. "No, Skye. That's not—"

She tossed the badge at him, a little too harshly as it bounced off his abs and landed on the floor. She shoved herself to her feet and moved away from him, putting as much distance between them as possible. Even covering her chest with crossed arms.

"I *do* care. That's the problem," he urged, slowly following her across the room. "I didn't expect to make any kind of connection with anyone. Tried not to, because of all this," he gestured to the computers.

The computer screens and multiple keyboards covering the small table looked like something out of a spy movie, a makeshift tech space with security cameras angled at all areas of the cabin's exterior. She hated it. What else had Guy—*Reed*—been watching while he was here?

What she thought had been a protector instinct was so much more. Much *worse.*

Everything about him felt like a lie. Even the kisses they'd shared. Down to the most intimate moments…

The kitchen... Our picnic...

Nausea started to replace her anger. Refueled it.

"There is nothing fake about you and me." He gave the admission softly, almost a whisper.

Those words hurt. Actually pricked her heart like an icepick. Her vision grew cloudy.

"But you're right," he continued, resignation taking over his face. He shoved his hands in his jeans pockets. "You should go. You'll be safer that way."

The pain etched across his face must have been done with the same icepick that had just stabbed her heart. They were tortured, cruel lines of anguish that he tried to cover with a resolute posture.

"Where will you go?" she dared to ask.

He shrugged. "I'll figure it out."

"Off to find another small-town waitress to screw?" The caustic words came out of her mouth before she could stop them. But it was the first thought in her brain. How many other waitresses had there been before her? How many stress-relieving escapades with a willing, naïve woman?

That wiped the expression from his face completely.

This was too much for her. Too much reality that was nowhere near as exhilarating as the suspense novels she'd read. It was nothing but confusion, pain, and pure rage.

"I know I don't deserve this," he began, in a subdued voice. "But please don't repeat anything I've told you to anyone. I have a big enough target on my back already."

"Who the hell would believe me?" she shot back harshly. She fiddled for her car keys from her pocket.

"You can't tell the sheriff either. Then these guys will know you were here. They have eyes everywhere."

Her throat turned dry. Not calling the cops would be a

crime. She'd seen two people shot and killed. Granted in self-defense, but still.

"Don't feel guilty about that," Reed pressed. "They were murderers; really evil men. I'm not just trying to keep myself safe, Skye..." His voice hitched. "I can't bear the thought of you getting hurt."

"Am I supposed to believe that *now* you actually care?"

She threw the door open and marched down the steps to her car. Not looking back was the hardest thing she'd ever done because she feared to see a blank expression on his face. If she did, he would see the tears pricking her eyes. Adrenaline was the only thing keeping her from crumpling on the rocks.

The stupid keys wouldn't fit in the ignition fast enough, and they dropped to the floor. She shoved them back in, and the engine finally started. The gravel slipped and flew across the ground as she turned her car around and sped down the driveway. Just before the bend, she dared a glance in the rearview mirror.

Through her misty vision, Reed stood on the porch in his bare feet, hands still shoved in his pockets. Looking helpless and—she couldn't be sure—dejected.

CHAPTER 16

PARANOIA REPLACED SKYE'S relentless tears halfway home, and she glanced through her rearview mirror more times than she could count. Every face was suddenly suspicious. A potential assassin that had witnessed the shit at Reed's cabin and had followed her every move. After several twists and turns—without using her blinker—she managed to make it home without anyone following her. She parked her car in the garage, turned off the engine, and sobbed into the steering wheel.

Her hands shook. Too much adrenaline from everything she'd seen.

So this was shock. She'd seen it in movies, described in books, but *living* it was completely different.

"Holy hell." She glanced at her reflection in the rearview mirror. Her barely-recognizable face was splotchy with red eyes, a complete mess.

She needed to call Sheriff Wyatt. Any decent citizen who'd just witnessed what she saw would call the authorities. He would know what to do. She grabbed her phone and stared at the screen. But her fingers wouldn't dial.

What about what Reed had said? The cartel had eyes everywhere and could find her. Hell, they'd found him. He'd asked her not to tell anyone, for her own safety.

She had no idea how Reed planned on dealing with those dead hitmen. Frankly, she didn't want to know. He was law enforcement, wasn't he? He knew how to handle things like that. This wasn't her responsibility. None of this was her concern, and she should take this moment to walk away. From all of it.

Her phone chimed with a text message.

Everything ok? from Nayanna.

"Shit." There was no way she could go back to the diner like this.

What do I tell them? If she didn't reply, then Ralph would get worried, and he *would* call the sheriff. Which would bring the cops to Reed's door in minutes.

Skye grimaced through texting a lie.

He wasn't there. But I don't feel well. Must have been Ralph's egg casserole. I'm going home to sleep it off.

Then she called Lynée. She answered on the first ring.

"Good morning, sunshine."

"Lynée?" Skye croaked.

"What's wrong?"

"I...He..." She could barely breathe through the words. "He's not real. It's not real." *Please, let none of this be real.*

"What do you mean? Are you hurt?"

"No, no. Guy didn't show up for work, so I went to check on him." She tried to block the images of the dead men out of her mind, to instead focus on breathing evenly. Focus on keeping her hands still. She relayed the events of that morning to her best friend, as calm as her frazzled mind would allow.

Lynée listened silently. When Skye finished, her friend finally asked, "Holy Moses. Are you at home?"

"Yes." *Will this woman ever curse? Even in a moment like this?*

"Hold on." The other end of the phone crackled, and a muffled voice came through. Followed by Lynée's softened response. "Okay, I'll be there in twenty minutes. Start a bath with that lavender bomb I gave you for your birthday."

"A bath? You're kidding, right?"

"You need to calm down, and warm baths are your favorite."

How the hell her best friend knew exactly what to say to make her feel better, Skye envied.

After locking her door and checking every window throughout the house, she finally felt quasi-comfortable enough to start a bath. As much as she loved them, she doubted the flowery-scented steam and bubbles would work to calm her nerves. This was true panic-attack territory. But what else was there to do?

She sank under the water, her whole head absorbed in warmth. Her rapid heartbeat was the only sound, and she focused on it. Trying to slow it down.

After a few seconds, she came back up and scraped her hair out of her face. When the tears threatened to spill again, she breathed in the lavender air. Having zero effect, she tried again. This time forcing her lungs to expand.

Breathe, Skye.

She inhaled several more times, the whole time thinking about Guy—Reed. She was falling in love with him, and now...

A knock on her door made her heart jump.

A moment later she heard, "It's me." Lynée's muffled voice came from the other side. They'd exchanged keys to each other's places as emergency backups. But that was pretty darn fast. Unless Skye had taken longer to draw her bath than she thought.

"Come in," Skye croaked.

The bathroom door opened.

Lynée's face peeked in, her smile genuine, but the concern was easily visible in her eyes. "Hey, chica."

Skye tried to smile back, but it felt more like a grimace. Honestly, though, seeing her face was soothing.

"I have lunch out here for you. Take your time. Come out when you're ready." She closed the door behind her. Moments later, music blared from her television in the living room, the uplifting and motivational channel she'd created for her workouts.

She'd lost count of how many songs passed while she was in the bath. When her fingers turned pruney, she climbed out and wrapped herself in her fluffiest towel. Then twirled her hair into a smaller towel piled on her head.

She stared at her reflection.

How did I let this happen?

Tears filled her red-rimmed eyes. *Stop it*, she scolded herself. He's just a man.

Well, this wasn't just *any* man. And the pain of the betrayal was enough to make her want to collapse to the floor.

She forced herself to leave the bathroom to get dressed. After donning her most comfortable pajama pants and an oversized sweater, she ventured into the living room. Her best friend had set takeout boxes on the coffee table, orange peel chicken ready for consumption, and two glasses of wine filled all the way to the top with a dark red. Despite the delicious smell, she had no appetite.

Lynée didn't say a word. Just walked over, wrapped her in a tight hug, and didn't let go.

The urge to cry threatened her again. But somehow,

the embrace kept her from losing it.

Eventually, she pulled back and wiped her face.

"I brought the Baldacci book."

Skye chuckled and then frowned. That was so Lynée. The book-junkie, who always brought a good read to cheer people up. Only now that particular book series just reminded her of Guy. Of *Reed*.

Which brought back all the horrible things she'd just witnessed.

"Come, sit. Drink and eat."

Skye obeyed, and just let her mind go numb and let her friend be in the driver's seat. The same thing Lynée had done all those years ago after the debacle with Vance. She'd always been like that. The sturdy rock Skye could cling to and feel secure again. They didn't even have to talk. It's like her friend knew silence could be just as comforting.

They turned on Netflix and watched episode after episode of a new comedy series. Until Skye fell asleep. Tucked there on the couch beside Lynée.

When she woke up, she was wrapped in her grandmother's quilt, still on the sofa. The sky had turned dark outside the window, and only the dim television lit the space around her. Lynée sat on the other end, her calm face watching the screen.

Skye sat up, wiping the sleep from her eyes. "What time is it?"

"Eleven. That was a great snooze. You must've really needed it."

"I'm amazed I slept at all. Did anyone call?" Maybe Reed had tried to contact her.

Lynée sighed. "Just Nayanna. Ralph was concerned you didn't come back. I told them you were sick and in bed. How do you feel?"

There were no words to describe how she felt. Fuzzy wasn't quite right, nor was tired. How does one describe a shattered heart?

"Empty," she finally said. "Scared."

On a deep breath, Lynée took Skye's hand. "Love is definitely scary."

She scoffed. "That's not what I meant."

"Isn't it?" she said softly.

Her mouth felt dry. She yanked the towel from her head and brushed her fingers through the still-damp strands. For some reason, it brought back the memory of Reed's hands on her skin after he'd walked in on her from her shower. The way her body felt alive at his touch, that unmistakable wanton flooding her senses. A way no other man had ever made her feel.

"None of it was real."

"Of course it was real," Lynée replied. "That much was easy to see."

"How can you possibly know that?" Her hands and feet felt cold; she pulled the blanket closer around her.

"The apple festival. It was all over his face. He never stopped looking at you. With that puppy dog, amorous expression. It was so cute, it was almost pitiful. Then how he handled Vance..." Lynée fanned herself. "That explains a *lot*."

Skye licked her lips. That was the moment for her. Back when he was just Guy the cook, she'd liked him a lot, fascinated by him. But the second she saw his protective side in a way that still tried to display manners and decorum, that was the moment she'd fallen in love with him.

"Chivalrous, a modern-day knight." Lynée cocked her head. "That's what I thought when I saw him. So if you say he was DEA, with the official badge and everything, that makes a lot of sense."

"What are you talking about? None of what happened at his cabin makes sense."

"Sure it does." The librarian grabbed her phone and pulled up a few articles. Then flipped her screen for Skye to read. "While you were sleeping, I did a little research after what you said, and found this."

She scanned the article, her eyes widening with every sentence. A listing of graduates from the DEA's Basic Agent Trainee class in Virginia several years ago, including one Reed Monroe. While there was no picture, it clearly stated his name. The next page she pulled up was a year-old article in the El Paso Times. It mentioned how a DEA agent was found deceased in a warehouse on the south side of town, believed to be a part of an investigation in a cartel's drug distribution operation. The murderer was still on the loose.

"It could be Reed's partner, but they didn't release the deceased's name." She handed back the phone.

"True, but then I looked up the truck he's driving. The license plate belonged to a man in New Mexico, who owns a tow-truck company right off Interstate-25. Straight up from El Paso."

"Your research skills are legendary."

"Librarians have more tricks up their sleeves than people realize. Combined with the internet, it's scary how much information I can uncover on someone. I'm just saying, his claims are not outside the realm of possibility." Wiggling her phone in the air, she added, "And do you know how many agents in this line of work are falsely accused of a crime?"

She bit her lip to keep it from trembling. "He shot and killed two people in front of me."

"In self-defense, and to protect you," Lynée whispered.

"What if he's a killer? One of those hired assassins?"

"He's law enforcement, Skye. A crusader."

Nerves amped up her heartbeat again. "Even if he really is, and every word he said was true…I can't do this. How could I possibly do this? It's too much."

Her friend's face was so calm. So collected, it was almost enraging to her. "You love him, Skye."

She opened her mouth to protest, but the words died on her tongue.

"You are the bravest woman I know. You're also the kindest. And more adventurous than this sleepy little town can offer."

"This sleepy little town is safe. And it's home."

"Sure it is. As long as you're not *hiding* here."

"I'm not hiding."

Lynée turned her body to face her more head-on. "What I'm saying is that life has dropped an adventure in your lap. Yes, it's way more than you were expecting, and it's scary. But what are you going to do about it? Sit in your house and hide?"

"It's shit-my-pants scary. Gunfights and cartels."

"That's not what I was talking about. I was talking about love. Nothing scarier than that."

Her mind became frazzled all over again, the same uneasy feeling as a hangover with no painkillers in sight. Her hands felt rough as she buried her face in them.

"All I'm saying is you will regret not putting yourself out there for him. For taking the *safe* road. You won't know for certain unless you try. If it doesn't work out, then you know we're always here. At least you tried. But you have to be willing to take that leap."

"A leap into fighting organized crime. With real bullets."

Lynée leaned forward, resting her elbows on her knees. "Something he's been fighting *alone*. Are you willing to let the man you love continue all by himself? While you sit here, safe in your living room?"

Skye bit her lip. Hell no, she was raised better than that. But this was truly next-level stuff and way over her head.

Her best friend took her hand. "Your self-defense course taught you how to prepare for situations that are unimaginable to most. They showed you different techniques and maneuvers, all of them urging you to *fight*. Fight back. Fight for what you love. Now's your chance to fight for what you love."

Skye slept like shit. Well, if she could call those last few hours sleep. Her head swam with images of Guy—Reed—fighting assassins at his home by himself. But not just that. Thoughts of his kisses, his arms wrapped around her, his playful teasing—God, she loved his playful side—filled her head until it ached.

She didn't know what she was going to do about him—them. But she had to talk to him. No doubt, he'd already left his cabin. He was probably on the road, hundreds of miles from this town. As he should be...

Thin wisps of sunrise teased the horizon, though much of the sky outside her window was dark.

She sat up suddenly. Her insides filled with warmth. She knew exactly where he was. No clue how she knew, she just did.

CHAPTER 17

REED OPENED HIS eyes, burning from a dead sleep. He'd be lucky if he slept for two hours. His whole body ached. Probably from all the adrenaline yesterday. He'd chastised himself all night about not telling Skye the truth sooner. But it had never been a question. He was never in one place long enough nor allowed himself to get close enough to anyone where he'd ever had to face this situation.

In the past, he wouldn't have thought twice about leaving and not looking back without an ounce of guilt. Hell, with anyone else he might've lied, just hightailed it out of there without a trace. It would've been easy to pretend not to care that she hated him.

But Skye was different. She was real and genuine, vivacious and compassionate, and she deserved the complete truth.

Dammit, she'd changed him. For the first time in a long time, he believed there was goodness in the world. He needed to believe that. Somehow she'd broken through his carefully erected walls. Made him believe anything was possible. Even living a regular life.

He never knew how empty his heart was until Skye. He'd just been a shell of a man living off the fumes of humanity long enough to finish his job. She reminded him he had a soul. A soul that now craved her blonde locks, blue eyes, and infectious optimism. Craved her touch.

The clock on the wall showed just before six a.m. He needed to get on the road before anyone found him here. The last thing he wanted to do was endanger anyone else. The sooner he solved this case, the sooner he could put all this chaos behind him. Retire this part of his dark life. Then, maybe... just maybe...

His thumb and index finger rubbed at his tired eyes. He was kidding himself. There was no way in hell she'd ever speak to him again, let alone consider being with him. This was the only thing his life was any good for. He just needed to suck it up and cut his losses. Even if that meant sacrificing his heart along with it.

The bell chimed over the front door.

Reed pulled his pistol from under the flimsy mattress, surged up from the cot, and hid behind the office door. He held his breath, waiting to hear the footsteps.

"Reed, it's me."

The sweetest voice in his totally fucked-up-world made his heart stop. He almost didn't want to turn the corner. Just in case he was dreaming. He couldn't bear that heartbreak, feeling her loss all over again.

He peered around the door.

Skye stood there in the diner's entryway, her mauve knit cardigan wrapped around her, held in place by her arms across her midsection.

"Hi." It was the only word that could manage past his dry throat.

She just stood there. Silent.

"How did you know I was here?" he asked.

A delicate shoulder lifted ever so slightly. "I just...knew."

He continued to hold his breath. A hundred more questions flashed through his brain, but he didn't dare speak. Too afraid that if he said more, she'd run.

"G—Reed, I was hurt. I mean, I know why you did what you did, why you came here, kept your identity a secret." She licked her lips. "But I still feel betrayed," she said softly. Her gaze dropped to the floor.

The remorse almost crippled him.

"I talked to Lynée." She took a step forward.

He figured she would. Hopefully, the librarian would know to keep their secrets. At least until after these cartel men were taken care of.

"What did she say?"

"She said not to let you go through this alone. That if I loved you, I should be by your side."

He swallowed hard at her words. *If she loves me... For the love of God and everything right in the world, please let that be true.*

"Then, I got to thinking about my mystery and suspense novels." She shuffled over and stood before him.

"What do they say you should do?" he asked, biting the inside of his cheek.

She huffed. "Well...first and foremost, the girl has to decide whether the guy is a hero or a villain. And if she should trust him."

He held very still, asking very softly. "And you asked yourself that same question."

"If you were one of the bad guys, you would've killed me already. Lord knows there were plenty of chances. Or you would've let one of the thugs finish me off. So, I think you're telling the truth."

He sighed.

Her head lifted to face him. "But Reed, have you told

me everything? I can't stand to think there's more hidden between us."

"Yes. Everything."

She stared at the ground again before holding his gaze. "My last question is... do you want to go through this alone? Or do you want me with you?"

The mixture of relief and fear that washed over him was inexplicable. He was so damn thankful she came to him.

He took her hand, hesitantly. Like if he used too much force, she'd vanish into thin air, and he'd discover this really was a daydream. But her smooth skin was warm, real. Right in front of him. "Yes. God, yes. I want you." He let out a small, reserved smile. "But I have a question for you. Lynée told you that if you loved me, you'd be by my side." He inhaled. "Do you love me?"

She bit her upper lip between her teeth. "Yes." Then her lips pulled into a smile. "Yes, I love you."

The quiet stillness between them filled his heart with a peace he'd never felt. He could barely believe those words from her lips. He'd never heard them from another woman before, and this was the only woman that mattered. He wanted to savor this.

He stepped closer, taking her other hand. "I love you too. I've never said that to anyone else before, Skye. That makes me all the more certain of them." He leaned down to kiss her sweetly. He rested his forehead against hers, breathing in her fruity scent. He loved the way she smelled, he loved the way she trusted him, and he loved the way she loved him. "I love you," he whispered.

She wrapped her arms around his neck. Lifting on her toes, she kissed him. Soft and slow, her salty tears falling between their lips. Tears of relief. Forgiveness.

God, please, let them be forgiving.

She pulled back from his embrace, and he wiped the tears from her cheeks. "Now that we've got that straight, we need a plan."

"We?" he asked.

"Well, yeah. You'll need my help."

He tilted his head. *Has she gone nuts?*

"Do you know where you're going? Another safe house somewhere, or just roughing it out in the woods?"

He took several seconds to answer. "I'll figure it out. But I won't let you get involved. It's too dangerous. We can't be together right now. I'll be on my way. Alone. When this is over, I'll come back."

Skye crossed her arms. "Oh, shut up. We don't have time for this macho, I-do-everything-on-my-own mentality. What do you need to solve this thing and stop running?"

Reed pinched the bridge of his nose. "I need a place to hook up my computer and finish my research. I just need a little more time. I'm so close to crackin' this thing, I can feel it. But I won't put you in danger at the same time."

She tapped her fingers against her elbow. All evidence of tears and vulnerability vanished. She was so adorable, playing detective. "We could hide you out at my place, but it's a bit cramped. And it's closer to town, so more people would see you." She worried her lip.

He shook his head. "You're not hearing me. No way. I'm not leading these animals to your doorstep." He stepped close, cupped the back of her neck in a possessive way, making her eyes widen. "I'm not losing someone else I love. It's not happening."

She stared into his eyes, her own misting over. "What kind of life will I have without *you*? No way am I sitting back doing nothing when I know you're out there fighting this by yourself. Don't you need some kind of cover?" She lifted her eyebrows.

He crushed his lips to her beautiful, plump mouth, begging her for understanding. He wanted to savor every waking moment with this woman. With those sweet lips against his, their hearts so close to each, his efforts were fruitless. How could he leave her behind?

Shit!

With a huff, he stepped back. "Fine. I hate when you're right."

"Okay then, we need to go somewhere they wouldn't know to find you. Someplace with an easy getaway and easy to blend in."

"Actually, easy to disappear." Reed smiled. "I have an idea. On the way, I need to show you a few things."

Her eyebrows pinched together. "Okay," she strung out the word.

He stepped closer, placing his hands on her hips. "Trust me, sunshine." He gave her a quick kiss. "I'm glad you came back," he whispered over her lips.

"You better be."

"Lynée, are you busy?" Skye cupped her cell phone while she closed the door of the back office. Ralph would be here any minute to open the diner, they didn't have a lot of time.

"Not at this time of the morning. Why are we whispering?"

"Nevermind that. I'm going to Seattle."

"Right now?"

"Yes, with Reed. He needs to finish his research, and we need to be away from Cascade Creek until he finds the guy who killed his partner."

"For how long?" Lynée's voice dipped with concern.

"I'm not sure. Hopefully, not too long." The sooner, the better. Her boss would be a bit pissed when she texted she had to take a vacation without notice.

"Look, I'm really glad you seemed to have worked things out with Reed. But this isn't exactly what I meant when I said fight for him. I meant to stay here and let law enforcement help solve everything. But you running off into hiding with him, Skye..."

"Trust me, Lynnie. Please. We have to do it this way."

A long pause came from the other end of the phone. Finally, after a sigh, her best friend replied, "Okay, babe. Be safe. Check-in with me every day."

Skye's posture softened. As long as she knew Lynée had her back, she could get through anything. "I promise. Love you, girl."

"Love you, too."

CHAPTER 18

SEVERAL HOURS WEST of Cascade Creek into the Snoqualmie Mountains, snow already topped the sharp peaks for late October. The crisp air blew Skye's hair away from her face through the slightly lowered window. Even though it was in the forties at this elevation, all the adrenaline going through her veins elevated her body heat. Reed pulled the truck onto a dirt path off the highway. Another mile in, they came to a clearing where a large pond glittered in the noon sun beside a natural berm. Thick bushes of snowbank flowers and towering pines backdropped the picturesque scenery.

Skye had never been to this part of the mountains. How in the world did this relative stranger to the Cascades know of this hidden gem?

Reed turned off the engine and grabbed one of the small duffel bags from behind his seat. "No one will hear us up here. Perfect spot to get in some practice."

"Um..." Warmth flushed her cheeks, remembering their picnic. "What kind of practice are you talking about?"

Reed bit his lip through a smile. "As amazing as that sounds, I was talking about something more practical." He opened the door and stepped out.

Skye followed him and crossed her arms against the

chilly breeze. The higher altitude was always a little jarring at first.

Reed dropped the bag in the grass and started collecting logs from around nearby trees. "I don't have any target sheets, so we'll have to make do with these."

Skye started picking up sticks to help.

"Bigger ones than that. Like this." He held up a big chunk of a tree branch. "I don't want to start you off with something too difficult."

"How did you know about this place?" She dropped the twigs and started looking for bigger ones.

"My uncle used to take me fishing here when I was a kid. It's also where he taught me how to shoot."

"Shoot what, exactly?" She followed him to the berm and handed him the wood one by one. He set them up along the natural wall, spacing them out with at least ten feet between each piece.

Then he opened the duffel bag.

He pulled out a small black case. Tucked inside a cloth was a black pistol. He gripped it easily in his hand and dug in the bag for clips. Already loaded.

"This is small enough for your palm. I want you to get comfortable shooting it."

"I don't think I need to do that."

Reed turned more sympathetic but still serious. "This is important. You need to know how to defend yourself."

Skye swallowed. She didn't miss the unspoken words...*against the cartel.* Or perhaps it was the implied possibility of him not being able to take them out himself.

He handed her the gun.

It was light. Lighter than she expected. Small enough for her tiny grip.

"It's empty. So don't worry about accidentally shooting

me. There's no clip. See?" He took her hand and turned it. Empty space filled the handle. "These fit inside." He held up the clip in his other hand. "When you load and unload, keep your finger off the trigger."

"Off the trigger," she echoed. Skye focused on the warmth of his fingers around hers. Along with his calm and steady voice, she could get through this.

He showed her the basics of loading the clip and snapping it into place. How to clear the weapon and release the clip. After several practice tries, she got the hang of it without pinching her skin. The pistol was a lot heavier with the loaded clip. He made her practice aiming at the logs against the berm.

Standing behind her, he braced his arm against her shoulder, helping her aim down the barrel's sights. His warm breath against her neck sent tingles down her arm.

"When you're ready to fire, take a deep breath, then squeeze the trigger on the exhale. Don't pull it. Just squeeze, nice and steady."

He stepped back.

The log through the sights was tiny. Her imagination was far too trained from her mystery novels, and she imagined a dark-hooded man aiming a weapon at her.

She fired.

A puff of dust rose up from the berm several feet off-target.

The recoil jarred her arm and set her heart racing.

"Not bad for your first shot," Reed commented behind her. "Use your core muscles to brace yourself against the recoil."

She fired again, and this one went several more feet off-target in the other direction. The casing flew up over her head, the metal bouncing off her hand and burning against her skin.

"Now you're compensating for the recoil. Expecting it and dipping the pistol in the other direction. Remember, just a light squeeze of the finger." He moved in behind her, gently pressing a hand into her shoulder. "Again. Breathe in, then fire." His whisper grazed along her neck, setting her pulse fluttering for a different reason.

Her third shot hit the top of the log, wood splintering into the air.

Skye allowed herself to smile. She glanced back at Reed.

He kissed the tip of her nose. "Keep going. You're on a roll." When he stepped back, she refocused and fired again. And again. Down the line, until she'd plugged a bullet or two into each log. Then he helped her practice reloading the clips with fresh bullets.

"If someone is coming at you, one shot out of this nine-millimeter won't do it. It'll take three or four shots. Or for someone bigger, you need to empty the clip into their chest. So, you'll need to practice firing back to back in the same spot."

Her heart stammered on that image. "Do you think it's going to come to that?"

"Probably not. But having the practice can't hurt." He helped her start reloading the clip. "Better safe than sorry."

"Um, this partner of yours..." Skye began, pressing the metal into the sheath. "Was he as good with a weapon as you?"

He paused for a long time, just watching her hands. "No. He was a much better shot."

"Hard to believe. Even better than what you did at the cabin?"

Reed scoffed. "He would've only needed one clip to

take down those thugs. Then again, he was also more seasoned."

"He was older than you?"

Reed checked the clip before he loaded it into the pistol, his face concentrated. Methodical. "Joe was the tactical part of our team. Front lines, if you need a term for it. He did all the face-to-faces with our targets." A hint of a smile crossed his lips. "Playing the part of a Mexican cartel druggie came easier to him. Fluent in Spanish and had a few family members in the drug scene. He once told me every time he had to meet with his contacts, he pretended to be one of his cousins. Who'd spent most of his life behind bars smuggling drugs into prison."

"And computers were your part of the team?" Skye aimed the gun at the log again.

"I came from computer forensics. My specialty was cybersecurity, and Joe convinced his superiors to recruit me from that department to join him on his case. He needed someone close by, hands-on, who could run the operation's tech part." His smile widened. "He chose me since I was the one who first cracked into the cartel's accounts and moved their money around for three months."

She lowered the weapon. "Seriously? How much money are we talking about here?"

"A couple hundred million." Reed grinned. "That wasn't even my directive." The look on his face was full of pride. An ego that she'd seen on him only three times before. First, after she tested his first bowl of clam chowder at the diner. Second, after he'd bested Vance at the festival. And again after their lovemaking, where he'd made her climax three times in a row.

Normally, an overinflated head was a major turnoff to her, but on him, with the millions of dollars, he'd hidden from criminals… So damn appealing.

"Why'd you do it?" she asked.

"Because I could. I heard my bosses complaining about the cartel leaders being a step ahead of them time and time again. The enemy had taken a giant leap forward in their technical capabilities. DEA couldn't keep up. So they put a contest out to our team. Find their shell companies and freeze their bank accounts. Winners would get a huge bonus and a case of tequila."

"And you won?"

"Yep. I tasted that first smooth shot of Cristalino right at my desk. Then took it a step further. I moved their money around. Had them chasing their cash around the globe like a cat on a laser pen."

Skye laughed at the image. She aimed again and went down the line of logs, plugging a bullet into each one. She missed about half of them and frowned. "Did they eventually catch up to you?"

"Several times. That's how I proved they had a more sophisticated tech person on their team."

"Which is when Joe asked you to join him?" She handed him the emptied gun.

He nodded, taking the weapon and clearing it. "The dynamic duo for three years. He'd find a lead, I'd follow it and give him everything he needed to confront the next target. All the while, I'd protect his back with surveillance, phone taps, the works. I got really good at hacking into GPS devices and putting trackers on cars. One of the few tasks I'd leave the safehouse for."

"You were stuck in the safe house the whole time?"

He reloaded the clip, bullet by bullet, taking a long time before he answered. His expression softened, the pride slipping from his gaze. "I didn't have as much field experience as he did, even though I'd been through the academy. Joe was extremely protective. Saw firsthand the carnage these bastards left behind. It's one thing tracking them down behind digital walls and screens. It's quite another to see the disturbing, bloody shit up close. He was trying to spare me that as long as possible." He started packing up the guns.

"You don't want to have a turn?" Skye asked, gesturing to the logs.

"Better to save the ammunition." He zipped the bag closed. "You're a quick study, Skye Winters. You'll be a sniper shot in no time." He grinned.

She sighed. Many of her shots went wide, and it would require a lot more precision to take down anyone coming at her. This was one activity she had very little faith in herself. "Maybe I'll just stick to moral support."

Reed stepped forward and curled an arm around her shoulders. He pulled her in for a gentle hug, placing a sweet kiss on her forehead. "You did great for your first time. This takes practice, like everything else."

She wrapped her arms around his middle, breathing in his cologne. Hoping it would soothe her a little more. He was way too kind. Trying to amp up her confidence. But she wasn't stupid. If thugs really were after him and his life depended on her ability to fire one shot when it counted, they were in serious trouble.

"You have no idea how great it feels to have you with me," he continued. "This whole thing will be over soon."

CHAPTER 19

DIEGO DOWNED HIS fifth shot of tequila. He'd bought a brand new bottle of his favorite to celebrate this night, supposed to be the culmination of his hunt for that *bastardo* DEA agent. Closing off that final loose end would prove to his uncle and all his generals that he was more than just a tech genius. That he could be trusted with the more strategic moves of their family's business. He was more than just a bastard child to burden the cartel with another mouth to feed. He was the next in line to take over everything.

But his plans had gone far left of his intended solution. More than twenty-four hours had passed, and those two jackasses he'd sent to Washington to take out the Hooverite still hadn't checked in. In this line of work, no news was definitely *not* good news.

His cell phone twerked across the dining room table. A blocked caller ID. This had to be them.

Diego scooped it up and answered. "What the hell took you so long?"

"*Diegocito.*"

His lungs froze. That tranquil voice did not belong to the scout. It belonged to his uncle.

"*Jefe. Que paso?*" Keeping his voice calm was well-practiced, despite his amped-up blood pressure.

"I hope I'm not disturbing you. You sound troubled."

Diego knew better than to trust the man's calm demeanor. Behind that cordial facade was something more brutal. Meant to throw people off their guard.

"Not at all. How is everything?"

"Come outside."

Diego stood, his heart rate now overloaded. He looked around, expecting two men to jump out of the shadows to throw a hood over his head. "You're here?" He forced his own voice to remain friendly. "Come inside for a drink, Tio."

"I have other plans tonight. So do you."

A knot crawled up his throat. The tequila threatened to expunge from his stomach in a violent escape. "I'm not dressed to go out, Tio. Perhaps tomorrow."

"Now." The line clicked off.

A harsh knock made him jump. His hands turned clammy, and the phone nearly slipped from his fingers. The sweat on his neck had nothing to do with the humidity.

He had no choice but to open the door. There was no ignoring Carlos Cabello. The more he delayed, the worse it would be.

He shucked the wrinkles out of his shirt and pants and brushed his fingers through his greasy hair. He'd just have to play this cool. Hopefully, his uncle had something else on his mind.

When he opened the door, Emilio stood on the stone porch. His uncle's head henchman leaned against the frame as if he was bored. The large brute always carried at least three weapons. And his disinterested air was nothing more than a cover. Calculating brutality was his whole existence. They merely tolerated each other.

Diego sent up a silent prayer that Emilio's ugly face wouldn't be the last face he ever saw on this Earth.

At the end of the pavestone walkway was his uncle's gray sedan. With the back door open, awaiting him. He doubted Carlos was inside. That man rarely met anyone outside his hacienda—too paranoid people would follow him. And he was right to worry. Diego had lost count of how many international agencies were looking for the cartel boss. He wouldn't be surprised if they had a whole satellite pointed at him right now.

Diego slowly approached the car, Emilio following closely. He also knew better than to ask him what his uncle wanted. Even if the second-in-command knew, he would never speak for Carlos Cabello.

Outside the car windows on the thirty-minute drive to his uncle's hacienda, all was quiet. Eery for the early evening, as if everyone knew the local cartel was out in force to pull in perceived snitches or to collect on loans.

What felt like only moments later, he stood before his uncle in the back of the hacienda. In the lion's den. The boss sat behind his ornately carved desk and sipped an expensive red wine. A soccer game played softly on the flatscreen television on the other side of the room, the announcer's voice providing a play-by-play accounting. He could almost hear the guy calling out the sequence of events coming up in this very room. Something similar to the killing by the barn a few weeks ago. Only with his own brains splattered across the handwoven rug under his feet.

Sweat dripped down Diego's spine, but he kept silent. His hands remained nonchalantly in his pockets. "*Buenos noches, señor.*"

"Actually, it hasn't been a good evening, *Diegocito*. But you already knew that."

"I didn't. How can I help make it better for you?"

"You can stop giving my men orders. I never approved

of them running errands for you."

His gut clenched. He wasn't stupid enough to think his uncle wouldn't find out he'd asked two of his thugs to go up to Washington State to remove that DEA agent. He was only hoping they'd be back by now with great news. "You've asked me to take care of the pest problem. That's what I'm doing."

Carlos slammed his fist on his desk. The sound echoed off the brick walls. "What you've done is caused me much bigger headaches. Your plan failed. Both my men are dead, and I'm now all over the radar in the Pacific Northwest." He grabbed a stack of papers from his desk and threw them at Diego. "Thanks to you and your stupidity."

Diego bit back a curse. He hated being called that name. He should've known his uncle sent scouts to find the whereabouts of his men. That was the only way he would've known the outcome before Diego. He caught one of the papers that slowly drifted toward the floor. It was a print-out of either a satellite image or a drone camera over a wooded area. Two bloody bodies lay outside a mountain cabin, with deep tire tracks leaving the gravel drive.

He forced a small smile to prove he wasn't afraid. "At least I found that bastard's location. I told you I would."

"And made him more untouchable in the process," Carlos bit back. "The man has already fled. You think you've actually helped me?" He scoffed and stood. Then started to prowl around the room. "I've killed men for lesser offenses, *cabron.*"

"Then do it." Diego put up his hands in mock surrender. "I've tried everything I can to make you happy."

"No. You've done everything you can to *surpass* me. To take control away from me. Because you think you could do it better?"

The danger behind the old man's words could've been measured by a bullet.

Diego forced a deep breath to calm his anger. "I've created a state-of-the-art distribution and communication system for you that no one will ever detect. I've ensured your security and secrecy for the next decade. All for you. And the only thanks I've received is more ridicule. More leashes. If I've pissed you off that much, then just do it. Better that than being a puppet you still see as a liability, instead of family."

Carlos scowled. In the dimly lit room, the shadows made him more formidable than he already was. "You are lucky I don't. You have my brother's face. And his impatience. What did I tell you all those years ago, *niño*?"

Fury flared up in his chest. "I am not a child!"

"Then stop behaving like one. Your time will come when you're ready. The only thing you've shown me, Diego, is that you are not ready. You still make careless mistakes caused by your arrogance. Mistakes I have to fix." He moved in front of his nephew and swiped his shoulders as if to clear the wrinkles.

Diego flinched.

Carlos' scowl turned to disdain. "You look like you just crawled out of a whorehouse. And you reek of that tequila—the sweet one." He grimaced. "Tomorrow, you'll go to *la casa del lago* while I clean this up. You will stay there until I tell you to return." He turned and stepped closer to the windows. Surveying his little fucked-up kingdom.

It took everything in Diego's power not to scream. *La casa del lago*. The hacienda at Lake Chalapa in southern Mexico was exile. Remote and disconnected, and where the cartel patriarch shoved aside problems until he could deal with them. It was the last place Diego wanted to go.

He followed him, clenching the paper in his fist. "No. I know where the DEA scum is. I will handle it myself."

"No!" his uncle bellowed. "You are to do nothing. Lay low, unseen."

"But what about the new system? My game launch needs to be managed to keep your mules up and running. Only I can do that."

"I am prepared to make certain sacrifices to ensure my business is secure. Including going back to my old methods for the time being. One of the most important lessons you will learn is when to strike and when to duck back into the sands. Like a scorpion. Come out too soon during sunlight, and you'll be scooped up by vultures."

"I can do this, Tio. I've worked too hard to disappear now."

Carlos whirled and wrapped his hand around Diego's neck. The grip suffocated him. "You will do as I say," he whispered harshly. "Disappear."

"Fine." The word scraped along his crushing vocal cords.

His uncle let go.

Diego gasped for breath and massaged his throat. Resenting every single one of the painful breaths, because they were all controlled by the son of a bitch in front of him.

The announcer from the soccer game bellowed out, "Goal." His uncle smiled at the television and started clapping his hands.

The sick bastard.

Emilio escorted Diego out, back to the gray sedan where another one of his uncle's men drove him back to his home. Diego kept his forehead against the glass window, willing the plan to formulate in his mind. He agreed, he would disappear.

But after. After he found that DEA *burro* and ended his life with his own pistol.

Once he made it back home, he'd track him down, follow the trail of desperation, and finish him off. He could get on a plane state-side easily enough.

He opened the paper in his fist. A name and license plate number scribbled at the bottom would lead him to the ultimate redemption: Guy Hancock.

CHAPTER 20

SKYE STARED AT the dilapidated motel through the windshield. Her stomach twisted at the exterior's fading paint, rusted-screened windows, and overgrown bushes. A forgotten, institutional look.

Charming.

Once they'd spotted the Seattle skyline driving in from the Cascade Mountains, they seemed to have driven for hours before they found this place tucked in the hills south of downtown. She'd hoped to keep Elliot Bay in view during their hideaway while Reed finished his research, so she could feel a little more at ease. The sound of the water always made her feel at home, knowing the creek was nearby. Yet these dense, dismal trees and down-trodden surroundings, now she felt truly on-the-run.

Out of her element.

Reed's confident, determined smile when he came out holding the keycard gave her hope.

She stepped out and grabbed one of the bags from the back.

He grabbed the rest from the other side. "We're all set."

"Are you sure about this place?"

"We need somewhere that takes cash without requiring ID." He gave the front door a sorry glance. "That limits our options."

"Which probably means their primary clients rent rooms by the hour," she mumbled under her breath. The place certainly looked like the kind that would cater to folks with prostitutes. Or drug deals. Not a place she would've ever expected to walk into her whole life.

But this is what fighting for what you loved looked like. Thick or thin, better or worse, good times and bad.

He led the way to their room, around the backside of the motel. At least they had an interior hallway, despite the flickering, dying overhead lights, and concrete floors. He swiped the keycard and swung open the door.

Small was the first thought that came into Skye's mind. Barely bigger than a walk-in closet with a heavy lemon cleaner smell that hung in the air. But it had a queen bed and a sturdy table on the far end, with a seventies-era floor lamp with tassels hanging down in the corner. The gray threadbare-carpeting looked from that decade as well.

"This will work for what we need." Reed set the bags on the bed.

"Are you sure this lighting is enough for you?" She moved to the back of the room and drew back the curtain. The orange-amber sunlight streamed through the screen-covered window. In the far distance, the dark waters from Elliot Bay peeked through the fall-colored trees. From this spot, she couldn't hear the water or smell its freshness, but at least she could *see* it. She finally took her first calming breath.

"We'll need to keep those closed," Reed answered. "We don't want any prying eyes." He turned all three locks on the door.

Skye gulped. A room with three deadbolts on a door was hardly comforting.

Reed moved beside her with an apologetic look. "I know this isn't what you're used to. But it's clean, out of the way, and will give me the time I need to find this guy." He pulled her into a hug. "I'm so glad you're with me. But if you want to go home, just say the word. I can—"

She shook her head at his shoulder. "No. I'm with you." She breathed in his cologne, the woodsy pine scent from their trek through the mountains. "Besides, this room is probably nicer than most places you've stayed in the last year. I can handle it." After a long, soothing kiss that settled her nerves, Skye started to unpack. "You set up your equipment, and I'll see to dinner. We'll eat, then you can start your manhunt."

"How did I get so lucky?" Reed wrapped his arms around her waist from behind, squeezing her tight. His breath tickled her ear as she reached behind her to caress his neck.

"Don't start that." She moaned when his hands moved up her front to massage her breasts. "Food first. We have a long night ahead of us."

"Promise?" he whispered in her ear. "I finally have you all to myself. You can hardly blame me for wanting to savor it."

She turned in his arms and kissed him. Her tongue dived deep into his mouth and tasted every morsel, stealing his breath. "That's an appetizer," she finally managed. "We'll have the entree later. Now, get to work, tiger." With a final squeeze of his fine ass, she continued unpacking.

By the time she finished, the whole table was covered with his laptop, hard drives, and more devices she didn't recognize. But Reed clearly knew what every piece of equipment was, where it went, and how he wanted it. And there were still more devices in the bag he hadn't yet set up.

"I thought I saw a seafood joint down the road on the way in. I'll grab some takeout and see if their clam chowder is better than yours."

Reed snorted. "You have a sick sense of humor." He reached into his back pocket and handed her a wad of cash. "No credit cards. Use a fake name and take a different route back."

"Done this a few times, haven't you?"

"Uh, yeah." His eyes widened. "Oh, wait. One more thing." He reached into the bag full of ammunition. He pulled out the pistol she'd practiced with earlier that day. "Take this with you."

She eyed it. "Is that really necessary?"

"Absolutely."

"I'm just going to get food. I'll be right back."

He slipped the thing inside a discreet sleeve and attached it to the inside of her waistband.

She pursed her lips, dreading the discomfort that thing would cause her back in the truck. What good would that thing be to her anyway? Her shot was shit.

He kissed her again, this time slow and patient. Reawakening the urge to take him right to bed. "I don't want to take any chances. You are far too precious to me."

"Prove that to me later." She grinned. Then he pulled the keys from his pocket.

When in the truck, her cheeks were still hot from his kiss. Despite the annoying pistol at her back, the ache between her legs practically begged for the promise later tonight.

"Easy, girl," she calmed herself in the rearview mirror. She drove down the road. "He's here to work. Not for a sexcapade." How in the world could she expect him to concentrate on his task if she was distracting him? Lord knew her own brain scattered like fireflies when he was around. All the messed up orders and unfilled coffee mugs at the diner since he started working there was proof of that.

She was here to support him. Keep him on track—and safe—until he found the ones after him. She'd do her best to keep him fed, hydrated, and hell, even motivated if she had to.

With two clam chowders, a salmon-and-rice dish, and jumbo crab cakes safely in an oversized bag marked "Halsey," Skye quickly locked the truck doors and scanned the parking lot. Maybe this runaway fugitive thing was affecting her more than she expected.

She nibbled on her lower lip as she took a different way back to the motel, just as Reed had instructed. It took longer, and she almost got lost a few times, but she managed to pull back onto motel property safe and sound. Even though she'd made sure to keep a watchful eye on the rearview mirror for followers, she seriously doubted the cartel could find them that fast and this far away from home.

The gun in her waistband was unnecessary, after all. Thank God.

With the keys in one hand and the takeout bag in the other, she returned to their room. When she opened the door, Reed hunched over the desk, adjusting some cords, his shirtless back facing her. The muscles in his shoulders bunched and tensed with every move, unbelievably enticing in the dim light.

She nearly swallowed her tongue right then. Keeping her hands off him would be next to impossible when he looked like that. Which meant, she would probably have a harder task during their stay than him.

He faced her and smiled at the bag of takeout food.

"That smells awesome."

Skye licked her top lip.

The man's abs turned her mind to jelly.

"Do you normally work shirtless?" she asked.

He glanced down at himself. "Setting everything up made me sweat. I needed to cool off."

She sidled past him, forcing herself not to touch him. She set the bag on the chair and dug in, needing to focus on something else.

"Skye."

She spun around. "Yes?"

"Is there something you want?" he asked as he stepped closer, brushing her hair off her face and resting his hands on her shoulders.

Warmth spread across her cheeks under his scrutiny. "Um, no. You have work."

His hands slid to her upper arms, bringing her closer. Her torso pressed against his strong bare chest. He leaned down to whisper in her ear. "I think there is something," he kissed her neck, "you're thinking about. Maybe you should tell me what it is. No more secrets between us." Another kiss.

Her breath came shallower as she shuddered.

"You're gonna have to tell me." Then he dropped his hands and stepped back.

Oh, no. She licked her lips again and closed the gap between them, resting her hands on his beautifully hard chest. "I...was just surprised to see you naked—without a shirt, I mean."

He chuckled.

She never had to spell it out. She couldn't say why she felt so shy about it, but damn, *asking* for sex? Her mother had taught her to be reserved, even play hard to get. But hell, she wanted it. She wanted Reed.

Shoving that shy and reserved persona to the side, Skye embraced a more courageous version of herself from somewhere deep inside. "Can you take a break from work?"

"All you have to do is ask." With a hand cupping her jaw, he leaned down to kiss her, guiding her tongue along his.

"Get naked with me."

He smiled before kissing her again, thoroughly, urgently as if she was his only hold on reality. He pulled the gun from her waistband and set it on top of the television stand.

"Hey. That's my gun."

He chuckled.

God, that sound. Deep and husky. It vibrated throughout her body, shooting straight to her sex.

He loosened her pants and then grabbed the hem of her shirt to pull it off. "I'll give you another gun, baby. I promise."

Her hands stroked his pecs, trailing kisses over every angel-blessed ridge and plane. She smoothed over his abs to his jeans, unfastening the belt and zipper. She pushed the garments down as he stepped out of them. Wrapping her fingers around his length, she savored the feel of silk over steel.

He groaned. Reaching for her bra, he unclasped it, adding it to the pile. "Lie down, baby."

In only her panties, she stretched out in the center of the bed, propping herself up on her elbows.

Reed leaned down to grab a condom from one of the bags and covered himself. Then his warm body hovered over hers, laying kisses on her, licking her neck, sucking her hard nipples.

She cried out as the electricity shot straight to her sex.

His fingers glossed over her mons, tunneling between her swelling nether lips. "Baby, I'm so glad you're ready because I can barely wait another second." He toyed with her clit a bit more, leaving her panting, before lowering himself over her.

She hooked her ankles at the backs of his thighs, waiting for him to join them as one.

"Please, Reed," she begged. She learned her lesson. *Ask, and ye shall receive.* And she needed to receive this very second before she exploded.

"Everything about you was made for me."

His words melted her remaining timidity. His body pushed into hers like she'd never felt what it was like to be with a man. She sighed with bliss. For her, being with Reed was like the first time. No man existed before him. Her heart and her body belonged to him. Perhaps for the rest of her life.

She had no clue how long their love-making lasted, but the sky outside had turned dark by the time her body squeezed around his cock in an intense climax. They finished together, their moans simultaneous.

Although Skye felt sated with his body on top of hers and tingles racing through her limbs, she didn't feel complete. Not nearly.

Her life had just awakened to something bigger. Brighter. Something she'd never experienced before. Being with this sexy and caring man was dangerous, certainly. But her heart just wouldn't listen. She'd crave him forever.

CHAPTER 21

DIM SUNLIGHT PEEKED across Skye's face through the top crease in the shabby curtain. She stretched her arms above her head and opened her eyes.

Reed still typed away on the keyboard, the screen flashing from one window to the next with three empty disposable coffee cups in front of him.

"Have you been at that all night?" she asked.

He rubbed his eyes and cracked his knuckles. When he turned in the chair to face her, her heart ached.

He looked like hell. Dark circles set up residence under his red-rimmed eyes, and the man desperately needed a shower.

"You didn't sleep at all, did you?" she deduced.

He shook his head. "What time is it?"

She glanced at the clock. "Just after seven."

He sighed, then winced as he stretched his neck muscles. "I need some more coffee."

Skye scoffed and threw the covers off her. "No, you need some sleep."

Reed's stomach growled audibly.

She chuckled. "Or how about some breakfast before you pass out?"

"That sounds amazing."

She stood and pulled on her jeans. "You hop in the shower, I'll go grab us some breakfast. Then you can get a few hours' sleep before you get back to it."

He came up behind her, the chair creaking as he stood and breathed in her scent off her neck. "You smell like sex and crabapple."

She giggled. "Don't start that. You need food." She turned in his arms and kissed him.

"What would I do without you?"

"Probably still be sitting in that chair after yet another crappy cup of coffee, your back aching, and your eyes going cross-eyed for the next forty-eight hours."

He kissed her forehead. "It's sad that's probably true."

She slapped him on the ass. "Rinse off that digital grime, and I'll be back in just a bit."

She grabbed the truck keys again and pulled her hair back into a messy bun.

"Take the gun with you," he added as he retreated into the bathroom to turn on the shower.

She scoffed. "Like the hardened criminals will be waiting for me at the coffee shop."

Reed didn't have the energy to push on the need for Skye to take the weapon with her. She looked so delectable all curled up in that bed, cozy and soft in just a tank top and panties. The urge to climb in beside her and have his way with her was so strong. But he truly could barely keep his eyes open.

He pulled on a fresh pair of clothes after his lightning-fast shower. The hot water barely worked at all on his tense muscles from sitting in that uncomfortable chair all night. His stomach rumbled again, protesting against all the rancid brew from the ancient coffee-maker in the room.

But his efforts were fruitful. Overnight, he'd found most of Daniel Huerta's history. Who he'd learned was actually Diego Huerta. His mother had died when he was a child—under questionable circumstances—and Diego went to live with his father's family in Mexico. No mention of a father on the birth certificate and much of his time south of the border wasn't documented either, but Reed could assume that's how Diego connected with the cartel. Through his father's family, somehow.

But this Huerta character was extremely efficient at covering his tracks. Which is why Reed hadn't gotten as far as he'd hoped overnight in finding the man's specific location. Normally, tracking someone didn't take him very much effort, their whole lives easily followed through records, social media, and banking habits. But Diego's information was like sifting through an ocean of haystacks where the needle kept moving and stabbing pinpricks through the straw. Huerta excelled at the life of a black hat cybercriminal. A damn good one.

But Reed was better. Only a few more hours, and he'd know where that murdering psychopath was, as well as see the look in his eyes as he watched his life crumble into ash.

Reed's year on the run was almost over.

He could barely wait to start his new life with Skye full-time. No more hiding, no more secrets. Just waking up each morning to her glorious smile, falling asleep beside her apple scent every night, and between those moments making her climax as many times as possible.

As he finished buttoning his jeans, a knock on the door pulled him from the bathroom.

"Did you forget the keycard?" He opened the door.

Not Skye.

The vicious sneer on the other side belonged to the same bastard who'd killed Joe.

Reed slammed the door, only for Diego Huerta to kick it back before it closed, missing Reed's face by mere inches. A silver gun glinted in the pale hallway lighting.

His training kicked in, and he knocked Huerta's arm to the side, dislodging the gun from his grip. The weapon sailed across the bed and clanked against the headboard.

Reed turned and lunged for the gun bag.

The man barreled into the room and tackled him like a seasoned linebacker.

All the air rushed out of Reed's lungs as he hit the floor. The television stand knocked over.

Huerta grabbed a chunk of hair on the top of his head and pulled his head back.

Reed winced and threw his elbow back, hoping to jab the guy somewhere painful. Like his jaw or temple.

Huerta hooked his arm around Reed's elbow, holding it at a painful angle at his side, immobilizing him.

"Judging from all the equipment on the table, you're the *bastardo* who made me chase my money around all those months." The man's voice was as cold as his hands pulling on his scalp.

All Reed could do was grimace through the pain.

"What do they know about me? Tell me, and I'll make your death quick."

"Fuck you," Reed gnarled.

"I can drag this out, make it so painful you'll beg me to kill you."

Reed could hear the smile in the monster's voice.

Huerta leaned closer to his ear. "How about I tie you to the chair, make you watch while I take little Miss Big Tits from behind, then slit her throat right in front of you. Will that make you talk?"

Reed thrashed against the restraint. The back of his head connected with Huerta's nose with a crunch. The man wailed and loosened his hold. Giving Reed just enough room to wrench free and roll out.

He clambered forward for the gun bag. Before he could get it open, Huerta surged forward with a knife.

Reed dodged out of the way, barely missing getting skewered in the gut.

Blood pouring from his nose, the man lunged again.

Reed knocked his hand away, and the blade skimmed his forearm, drawing a thick line of blood. The knife flung out of the guy's grip and clattered against the wall.

The two men started throwing punches, blocking each other's fists with equal force. Huerta landed several vicious right hooks to Reed's obliques. He cringed away, protecting his right side. Every punch he threw barely affected his opponent, and his strength waned, while the enemy seemed to gain power with each swing. He launched a jab with his left hand.

Diego blocked it easily and countered with an uppercut to his jaw.

The room tilted in an agonizing spin, and everything darkened. Flickerings of bright light circled in front of him as he threw his arms out to catch his fall. He stared up at the ceiling as it continued to spin, and his head exploded in pain.

A vision of Skye's angelic face blurred in and out of focus, only to keep morphing into Huerta's vicious sneer standing over him.

Intense pressure closed off his throat, and Reed gasped. But no air filled his lungs. He clawed at his throat, only to feel knobby fingers gripping tightly. Squeezing the life from him.

"You're as useless as your partner, you DEA scum."

Reed bucked his hips, trying to throw the man's balance forward so he could get free. But the vice grip only tightened more. He choked and gagged. Tearing at the hands at his neck to pry them off.

He had to protect Skye.

Skye.

The room tunneled into a tiny speck of light at the end.

After all this, he couldn't help anyone. Not even himself.

CHAPTER 22

WITH A TAKEOUT bag in one hand and a tray of two steaming coffees in the other, Skye didn't think twice about the door sitting slightly open when she returned to the motel. Reed knew she was coming back and was just being thoughtful.

She wedged the door open with her elbow.

Coughing and gasping noises didn't match with what she expected to see. Someone leaned over another form on the bed. Choking them.

Her mind finally recognized the form was Reed. His eyes bulged from their sockets, and his face was a purplish-blue.

She gasped. The bag slipped from her hand.

The stranger looked over at her.

His eyes were sickly cold. Blood streamed from his nose.

Her stomach turned to solid metal and plummeted into her ankles.

Before she could finish processing the horror in the room, the man let go of Reed and charged at her.

Skye flung the hot coffees at his face, hoping to blind him. He wailed at the burning liquid, giving her enough time to lunge for the gun she'd left on the television stand.

Only it wasn't there. It had been knocked over.

The pistol lay on the floor beside the trash can.

Her fingers grasped the handle just before the man slammed her body into the wall. He wrapped an arm around her to reach for the gun, but she elbowed him hard in the groin.

He recoiled back with a howl.

She spun and aimed the gun. Her hands shook as it fired.

The first shot rang in her ears. She had no idea where the bullet landed, but the stranger stumbled.

"*Puta madre!*"

Out of the corner of her eye, she saw Reed still laying on the bed, rubbing his neck, gasping and coughing.

The madman pounced on her. She fired again, but he knocked the barrel to the side with a flick of his hand. The gun landed on the floor, out of reach. His arms wrapped around her again, like a vicious bear.

She raised her arms to shove the heel of her palm up into his nostrils.

The crunch beneath her hand made him scream. Fresh blood poured from his nose.

She fought the urge to vomit from the smell of the blood combined with her overwhelming fear and dashed over to Reed. But the monster caught her from behind and pulled her in, her arms barred at her sides.

With a growl, he lifted her up.

Her legs flailed in the air. She screamed and threw her head back, hoping to land her skull against his nose. But her head merely grazed off his.

He put her down to readjust his hold and reach for something.

Her gaze caught the glint of a knife in the guy's hand.

She froze. The cold blade slipped under her neck. She winced, the sharp edge threatening to slice her skin.

"You're a fiery one, aren't you? I'm going to make this hurt, *puta*. When I'm finished, no one will be able to recognize you, that is if they can find all the pieces."

Tears stung her eyes, and her whole body shook. There was barely any space in her mind to realize Reed had been right. The cartel found them so much faster than she imagined.

All of this was real. Pieces of her life flashed before her—her parents, Lynée, and fantasies of she and Reed together. This horrible, gut-wrenching nightmare was real, and there'd be no waking up.

"Let her go," a harsh voice croaked.

One she didn't recognize. It was rough, hoarse, almost like from a swamp creature in a bad movie.

Reed stood at the end of the bed. Aiming a gun. A gash marred the side of one arm.

The man shifted Skye in front of him, blocking Reed's shot. The knife pressed harder into her neck.

She whimpered. Reed's face was still an awful mixture of blue and purple, and red dots splotched the whites of his eyes.

"I'll slice her pretty neck...cut out her tongue and wag it in front of you. Put down the gun."

Everything in her body turned numb with fear. Somehow in all the panic and chaos slamming into her brain, a moment of the self-defense course flooded her memory. The instructor had grabbed her from behind, just like this.

Make yourself heavy.

Her mind struggled to remember. But with the blade still against her neck, going limp right now would only use her body weight to slice her own throat.

"Let her go, Huerta," Reed rasped, "and I'll let you walk out that door. Otherwise, you're a dead man. Those are your only options."

"No, they aren't," he chuckled right into her ear. "I can drag her with me. Have some fun with her." He stepped back, pulling her with him. The blade tucked into her skin, and she had no choice but to move backward too.

Tears slipped from her eyes, the cold trail slowly moving down her cheek. Followed by more tears. She had to get out of his hold. Somehow. If only he would just...

"There's nowhere you can go I can't find you. And Dark Inferno is already compromised. A useless tool for the cartel now. By the way," Reed smirked, "The graphics on that thing are pathetic. Your coding is sloppy."

Huerta's breathing increased in her ear. "Better than anything you can do. And we've already moved on from Dark Inferno." He pointed the knife at Reed. "You all are so slow, you're obsolete."

This was her signal.

She went limp. Then dropped to the ground. Her body slipped from his hold.

A shot rang out, a loud boom that echoed off the walls.

Skye screamed and covered her ears, ducking away.

A gurgling noise made her look up.

Huerta dropped to his knees, the knife thunking on the carpet. Reed's bullet had gone straight through the man's neck. A large hole oozed bright crimson blood down onto his shirt. Gravity carried him forward, and he face-planted directly next to Skye.

She glanced over at Reed.

He lowered the gun to his side, his chest heaving with each breath as he stared back at her. Somehow, she made it to her feet and scrambled over to him. He squeezed her back so tightly, and all she could do was hyperventilate into his shoulder.

"Are you okay?" he asked. His raw voice scratched like sandpaper.

"God, I don't know. What about you?" She caressed his face, careful not to touch his neck. The skin was already covered in vicious bruises. His splotched eyes looked so painful. The gash still oozed blood, slowly. "You need a doctor."

"I'll be okay. We need to get you a bandage."

"Me? Why?" She touched her throat, and when she pulled her hand back, blood smeared her fingers. The knife had dug in a little too tight. "It doesn't even hurt."

He let out a weak chuckle, then grimaced, holding his side. "It will. Adrenaline is still pumping through you. Nice shot, by the way." He nodded to Huerta on the floor.

Skye looked at the man lying lifeless on the floor, his blood still pooling on the carpet. She stepped back, hands instinctively covering her mouth, and a shriek escaped like she expected the man to move any second. Tears streamed down her cheeks.

Reed stepped closer, cupping her upper arms. "You're shaking. You're going into shock."

She could only stare at him, the events of the last few minutes replaying on a loop, over and over in her head.

Reed pulled her close, rubbing her feverishly as if he could calm her tremors.

"I was so scared. Seeing you," she sobbed aloud, her voice trembling, "seeing you on the bed, him choking you." Her head tipped onto his shoulder, letting the intensity of what she just went through pour out.

He kissed her hair. "Ssh. It's over, baby. You saved my

life. And it's over." He kissed her forehead again, holding her as she balled over the extreme fear. "Deep breaths. It's a reaction to shock; your blood vessels constrict during the fight-or-flight response. Which limits the amount of oxygen they hold. This feeling will pass, just keep breathing."

After several moments, her sobs finally ceased. She wiped her eyes and looked at the man she almost lost. "I'm sorry."

"Don't be." His hands holding her arms, he stepped her back to the edge of the bed to sit. "Sweetheart, the cops will be here any second, and we can't be found here. I need to pack our stuff."

She nodded. Hating feeling like a helpless person prone to panic attacks, but loving that Reed was close to comfort her.

In several quick minutes, Reed had the place packed, and with a towel, gave the table and chair a quick wipe-down so police couldn't find useful fingerprints.

Her trembling increased when he wiped off Huerta's hands as well, taking a plastic fork from the takeout bags in the trashcan to clean under the man's fingernails.

"What are you—"

"My skin might be in there."

Skye covered her mouth and turned away. She couldn't think about that.

Do something. Help him.

She grabbed another towel and wiped down the bathroom counters, toilet handle, and shower stall. Anywhere they might have touched.

Reed grabbed the pistols and his knife from the floor, as well as Huerta's blade, marred with streaks of blood. Hers, probably Reed's too. He stashed them in the side pocket of one of his bags, then stripped the comforter from the bed.

"Ready?" He touched her shoulder.

"Yes."

"Ok, babe. Can you carry this?"

She took the comforter and a bag and followed him to the door.

"Let me go first," he whispered.

She stepped back as he opened the door and scanned the hallway. "Clear. Let's go."

They both moved down the stairs and out a back service door, stopping periodically to scan the surroundings.

They loaded everything in the truck, and Reed retrieved a cell phone from his overnight bag. "Here, baby, power this on, call 911, and tell the police there's an unconscious man in room 802."

She made the call, quelling the acid that bubbled in her stomach at just saying the words out loud. Before the operator asked any questions, she hung up.

They got on the road, heading toward the city. A mile down the hill, he pulled into a parking lot. Instead of turning into a spot, he stopped beside a commercial trash can. "Hand me the phone."

She turned it over, where he proceeded to snap the phone in half, then opened the window and pitched it. The comforter from the bed followed into the bin.

Then Reed made a U-turn to make their way higher up the mountain, into the pass. They drove aimlessly for a while, she couldn't be sure how long since she'd kept her eyes closed most of the drive, trying to breathe deeply to overcome the nausea that had gripped her ever since that horrible experience in the motel.

"How you feelin'?"

She opened her eyes. Tall trees lined the road on either side, and they were clearly much higher up in the pass than she expected. "I'm okay."

"Are you hungry?"

Her stomach was still too unsettled to even think about eating. But maybe some toast would soak up the fear. They hadn't eaten the breakfast she'd brought back. She remembered carrying in that bag of burritos and hash browns to refuel him after such a long night of working, and she'd actually smiled, feeling so proud of him. Then their whole words were flipped upside down. She wondered if she'd smile ever again.

He reached over and cupped her hand. "A few miles up the road, there's a cafe, we can grab a bite. Get you some water or coffee."

"How are you so calm?" she asked his reflection in the window. His eyes still unnerved her, with red splotches so easily visible even in the glass.

It was a long moment before he responded. "I've been doing this a while."

Reed watched Skye carefully in the booth at the cafe. After he cleaned up his arm in the bathroom and wrapped it with some paper towels, he slid in beside her on the cushion to hold her if she started shaking again. She just sat there, stirring a cup of coffee and staring at the swirling liquid. The dazed expression she wore is what rattled him most. He hated seeing her like this. And it was completely his fault.

At least she'd downed half the glass of water. But she hadn't touched her toast.

"You did great back there, baby."

"What do you mean? I missed him, didn't I?"

"You got him in the leg."

She scoffed. "A lot of good that did. He still managed to get a knife on me. My hands were shaking so much, I was sure I missed him."

Reed kept his voice low. "The second he moved the knife, you knew exactly what to do."

She finally looked up at him. Her face was so pale, but damn, her eyes were so beautiful. Even now. "I took a self-defense course. Shortly after the Vance thing." She swallowed hard. "Lynée urged me to take it. That was the first move they taught me."

"Thank God for that. It's a shame you had to learn those maneuvers at all, but it made all the difference back there."

Her eyes misted over. "You've been on the run and on your guard so long. A whole year. When did you start being able to breathe again?"

He caressed her cheek. "When I met you."

Skye leaned into his hand, and the corner of her mouth lifted ever so slightly. "Please tell me with that man gone, now you're free."

He nodded. "That bastard killed Joe. Now I can prove it and clear my name."

"So, where do we go?" She leaned her head on his shoulder. Just sitting there side by side in a booth, like a normal couple.

He couldn't hide a hint of a smile on his lips. "I take you home." He wanted that so much.

Normal.

"Then..." Her sigh was shaky. "What happens to us?"

He gripped her hand in his, fluttering kisses along her knuckles. "I'd like to try a full-time boyfriend with you. Up here in the mountains. Eventually, more than that. If you're interested."

Her eyebrows raised, and for the first time since they left, he saw that glimmer of life. "Really? You're not interested in continuing to be an agent?"

He shook his head. "Definitely not. You're what I want."

She smiled.

There it was. What he dreamed of most nights. That angelic face all lit up, staring at him.

He laced his fingers in hers. "For the time being, unless you're in class or with family and friends, I don't want you out of my sight. In fact, I'd be completely fine with you in my bed twenty-four seven."

She straightened in her seat. "Your bed? No way, we are *not* going back to that place again. Remember, *your* place was shot all to hell with a few dead carcasses lying around. We're going to *my* bed."

"Sunshine, watch yourself," he said with a grin, narrowing his eyes. "I recall three different instances in which you needed a spanking. Should we make it four?" His eyebrow lifted.

Her eyes may have widened, but the sparkle told him *that* was exactly what she wanted.

CHAPTER 23

THE FIRST CALL Skye had made when she returned home to Cascade Creek was to Lynée. Her worry and relief were easily heard through the phone with tears and sobbing. Even Reed had winced. She'd spilled the entire ordeal to her best friend.

After a painfully long pause, Lynée made her swear never to run off like that again.

An easy promise to make.

The good news was the imminent threat was over. Reed had the proof he needed. There was no need to run anymore.

Finally, the pair of them could get back to normal.

Only she had no idea how long it would take her to get used to calling him Reed Monroe, not Guy Hancock.

Skye and Reed returned to the diner Tuesday morning for their regular shifts as if nothing had happened. He looked like hell, and she sported a fresh bandage on her neck. At least his high-neck sweater covered most of the bruises on his throat. Those would be really hard to explain.

The Halloween decorations of fake spiderwebs in the corners and hanging rubber bats from the ceiling were replaced with fall leaves twisted in garlands and wreaths hanging in the windows. The jack-o'-lanterns were replaced with fresh, painted pumpkins on the counter ends. Everything from the Autumn decorations boxes she'd packed away last year.

The fact that her boss had managed to turn over the decorations while she was away gave her a sigh of relief. Things weren't completely falling apart without her, despite the bad food. Even if he hadn't put them up himself—he wasn't the decorating-type—at least he'd known to ask others to update the ambiance.

Nayanna gave her a big hug, her bright smile so comforting. Of course, she had lots of questions. But from Ralph's glare and crossed arms from across the counter, the chatter stopped.

"I see your stomach bug finally improved," he said. From his tone, clearly, he didn't believe that story.

Skye glanced around the nearly empty diner. "I see your cooking hasn't."

He fisted his hands by his sides. "Really? You leave with no warning and no one to cover your shifts for several *days*, and you think it's a good idea to insult me?"

She gave him a sympathetic smile. "It's a long story, a super boring one. One day, we'll explain it. All we can say is...we're sorry. It won't happen again. To make up for it, I'll make extra pies all week. And I'll be sure to tell everyone you're fully staffed again, so they can come back."

"I should fire you, you know that?"

Skye nodded. "And I would deserve it."

Reed stepped forward. "It's my fault."

She stopped him with a hand on his shoulder. Then looked at her boss. "If you don't fire us, then you won't have to cook anymore."

His jaw flicked. He was giving in. He'd stew in his

anger for a day or two, but then he'd get over it. "Extra pies all month."

"Done." She gave him a sideways hug. "And you did a wonderful job on the fall decorations, by the way. I'll bring in some fresh flowers for all the tables, too."

Ralph grunted and gave Reed the side-eye as he walked past.

The rest of the shift went by quickly. Word spread fast throughout town that Ralph wasn't cooking, so the lunch rush picked up. Everyone was too busy to pressure her or Reed—still Guy to them—to explain what happened. She was grateful Ralph had given both of them the silent treatment for the rest of the day.

Despite the packed place, she'd make her way back into the kitchen any chance she had to see Reed. To touch him or give him a hug from behind. Probably her own subconscious way of making sure he was still real. That they weren't still back in that Seattle motel room dead on the floor.

Customers kept asking her about her neck. Using a move from Reed's playbook seemed like the best approach. "Had a fight with the curling iron," she told Gloria and Victor. Then Tom and Sylvia brought it up, to which she replied, "A witch placed a curse on me for having a bad singing voice."

Lynée arrived during her lunch break, as her normal routine. Skye nearly burst from every pore. She squealed through a huge hug that lasted much longer than normal. Ralph eventually cleared his throat loudly from behind the counter, and she went back to work. Her friend took her usual stool and perused a magazine while she waited.

Just after lunch, a motorcycle engine rumbled outside the diner. Skye was used to hearing motorcycles ride through town, but it was rare to see one shining so brightly in the parking lot that the glare would nearly blind her behind the counter. The rider didn't look familiar either. All she could see from her angle was the black riding boot pushing down the kickstand.

Lynée held up her Windsor Fashion magazine at Skye. "Which one do you like better—this one or that one?" She pointed to two different tweed blazers on the page.

"Really, sweetie, don't you think you can branch out a little? Something different from these conservative clothes? These are for old ladies."

She furrowed her brows. "It's scholastic. Makes one look distinguished and intellectual."

"You mean, bookish?"

"Well, then that would be fitting for me, wouldn't it?"

Skye wanted to roll her eyes but didn't want to hurt her friend's feelings. She flipped a few pages forward and pointed to a pretty V-neck sweater, much lower than Lynée would normally wear. "That one is beautiful. Care to be a bit more adventurous?"

Lynée frowned and looked over her reading glasses at Skye. She kept her voice lowered so others wouldn't hear. "You mean adventurous like you? Running off with a vigilante DEA agent leaving behind gunfights and a mountain of rumors?"

Skye smirked. "It's a sweater, Lynnie. Not a prison sentence."

Lynée opened her mouth to fight back, but the man on the motorcycle strolled in.

Dark sunglasses matched his black leather jacket and boots. His brown beard and mustache gave him a rugged look that seemed to coincide with the personality of the chopper outside. He surveyed the rest of the tables throughout the room, taking his time to look at each customer. Then he sat at the counter, his large frame barely fitting on the narrow chair. Slipping off his leather jacket and draping it over the back, the tattoos on his arms accentuated his impressive muscles beneath the black T-shirt—biceps bulging and triceps flexing.

If Skye wasn't so deliriously happy with Reed, she could see breaking a few of her rules with this man.

"Hey, stranger. Welcome to Rock Road Diner. What can I do ya' for?"

He removed his sunglasses, revealing intense brown eyes. Confident, almost mischievous. But what struck her most was the intensity behind those irises, like he held a mountain range full of secrets. That was perhaps about to come crumbling down on someone.

With his forearm resting on the counter, he gave her a determined look, much too pleased with himself. "I'll take a black coffee, a turkey club on wheat," he paused and shifted his head to look behind her. "And that man right there." He pointed at Reed through the kitchen window.

Skye froze.

Even Lynée looked up from her magazine in shock.

This man didn't look like he was from the cartel. If he was here to hurt Reed, he certainly wouldn't have made his presence so blatantly obvious to everyone in the room.

Reed stared curiously at the stranger.

She carefully moved behind the counter to pour the customer's black coffee. "What do you want with Guy?" she asked him, sliding over the mug.

But his attention was wholly focused on the cook. "Reed Monroe, you're under arrest."

Read the continuation in Renegade

A MESSAGE FROM THE AUTHORS

*Thank you so much for reading Runaway!
We hope you read the continuation and finale of the series
in Renegade.*

*If you enjoyed this story, please consider posting a review
at one or more of your favorite retailers, as well as
Goodreads. Even a short review, one or two lines, can be
a tremendous help and encouragement to the authors.
Your review is also a gift to other readers who may be
searching for just this sort of story,
and will be grateful you helped them find it.*

Thank you!

Mia London & Susan Sheehey

Cascade Mountain Manhunt Series
Runaway
Renegade

Other Novels By Mia London

Sweet Escape Series
Dry Spell
Hot Spell
Cold Spell

Undeniable Series
Undeniable Fate
Undeniable Love

Perfect Series
Perfect Seduction
Perfect Surrender

Life To The Max
Wanton Angel (Prequel to Life To The Max)

Beyond Lace (Hard Men of the Rockies 4)

Accidental Tryst

Other Novels By Susan Sheehey

Sweet Escape Series
Dry Spell
Hot Spell
Cold Spell

Royals of Solana Series Boxset
Prince of Solana
Jewel of Solana
Crown of Solana
Royal Wedding novella

Knights of Texas Series
Tell Me What You Want
Tell Me What You Crave
Tell Me What You Need
Tell Me What You Feel

Audrey's Promise

Summer Heat: Imperfectly Yours Anthology

ABOUT THE AUTHORS

Mia London

Mia London loves to write.

After reading fiction for years, she decided it was finally time to put those images and scenes floating around in her head down on paper.

She is a huge fan of romance, highly optimistic, and wildly faithful to the HEA (happily ever after). Her goal is to create a fantasy you will enjoy with characters you could love.

She lives in Texas with her attentive, loving, supermodel husband, and perfectly behaved, brilliant children. Her produce never wilts, there are no weeds in her flowerbeds, and chocolate is her favorite food group.

http://www.facebook.com/MiaLondonAuthor
http://www.twitter.com/MiaLondonAuthor
http://www.goodreads.com/author/show/8414916.Mia_London
MiaLondon.com
Email: mia@mialondon.com

Susan Sheehey

Susan Sheehey writes contemporary romance and romantic suspense adventure. Water plays a crucial element in all her novels, and she's a strong advocate for autism awareness and acceptance. She squeezes in writing time between chauffeuring around her two boys and guzzling down French vanilla coffee. Her beloved husband keeps her relatively sane and full of laughter. She and her family live in Texas.

SusanSheehey.com
http://www.facebook.com/SusanSheehey
http://www.twitter.com/SusieQWriter
http://www.bookbub.com/authors/susan-sheehey
http://www.goodreads.com/author/show/7189847.Susan _Sheehey

Join her newsletter for monthly announcements, updates, and special giveaways here:
https://landing.mailerlite.com/webforms/landing/p5b0i9

Interested in Advance Reader Copies of Susan's upcoming novels?
Let her know here:
https://www.SusanSheehey.com/Contact